LISA SUZANNE

GRAND SLAM
VEGAS HEAT: BASES LOADED
BOOK FIVE

Published in the United States of America by Books by LS, LLC.

ISBN: 9798884009486

Vegas Heat
Grand Slam

Books by Lisa Suzanne

VEGAS HEAT: THE EXPANSION TEAM
Curveball (Book One)
Fastball (Book Two)
Flyball (Book Three)
Groundball (Book Four)
Hardball (Book Five)

VEGAS ACES
Home Game (Book One)
Long Game (Book Two)
Fair Game (Book Three)
Waiting Game (Book Four)
End Game (Book Five)

VEGAS ACES: THE QUARTERBACK
Traded (Book One)
Tackled (Book Two)
Timeout (Book Three)
Turnover (Book Four)
Touchdown (Book Five)

VEGAS ACES: THE TIGHT END
Tight Spot (Book One)
Tight Hold (Book Two)
Tight Fit (Book Three)
Tight Laced (Book Four)
Tight End (Book Five)

VEGAS ACES: THE WIDE RECEIVER
Rookie Mistake (Book One)
Hidden Mistake (Book Two)
Honest Mistake (Book Three)
No Mistake (Book Four)
Favorite Mistake (Book Five)

Visit Lisa on Amazon for more titles

Dedication

To my favorite three.

Chapter 1
Danny

The flashes of the cameras are literally blinding. I keep my head down to give her the spotlight, but she tugs on my hand as if she needs me beside her.

I glance up, and I smile.

Of course I smile.

I'm nervous as fuck. I'm not used to this level of attention, though I'm no stranger to the paparazzi.

I need her to know I'm right here, so I clutch her hand tightly. She squeezes mine back as she smiles and waves, her pop star persona firmly back in place.

It's a side I've only seen glimpses of—and never from this perspective.

It's still her underneath the façade, but the wide smile doesn't quite reach her eyes the way it does when I've said something to make her laugh.

It's only now that I see how very well I know her. These people here *think* they know her, but all they know is what she's allowed them to see. All they know is the veneer she or her dad or some combination of the two have crafted.

But I know her heart. Of course I do. Because when someone's meant for you, your hearts speak a language nobody else could ever understand.

And I know damn well that Caroline Alexis Bodega is meant for me. I think I knew that somehow intrinsically before I ever met her. There's a deep connection pulling us together, and we will not allow anybody to break that.

They'll try.

Her dad will try.

Brooks will try.

Maybe even her fans, though I can't imagine they'd want us apart when they see the genuine smile on her face as she looks up into my eyes.

Like she's doing now.

I see the anxiety there, the silent conversation to look to my left, and I do. I spot her father standing beside Brooks, and they both look like they're going to bust a vein in their foreheads even from here, even with the bright lights and the constant flashes attacking us.

We make our way up to the *step and repeat*—the series of panels with the logo for tonight's event repeated over and over across a series of panels where the stars can come tonight to have their photo taken.

I step back to allow my beautiful wife to take photos solo first, and then she nods toward me, and I join her for our first official public photos.

I slide my arm around her waist, and she leans into me. I can't see her face since we're both looking at the cameras, but I know her smile is wide.

She glances up at me, and I look down at her, and I know the photo is captured of the loving look we're sharing.

It'll spark a million rumors. The Bodegiacs will be going crazy trying to figure out this latest puzzle. Is she working with the Vegas Heat? Is she leaving her management company? Did she have a falling out with her father—the man who, at least according to the entire world, is her hero, her closest ally, her best friend?

It's not a puzzle at all, though.

It's simply true love.

After we smile for the cameras, we step down. We're escorted into the building to a room that's not too far from the stage. A placard on the door lets us know which one is for Alexis.

Standing just outside the door is Gregory.

Alexis runs into his arms. "I'm so happy you're here!"

"Wouldn't miss it for the world, ma'am." He gives me a nod over her shoulder, and I nod back politely.

The assistant leading us opens the door for us, and Brooks and Alexis's father are waiting in the room.

Her father turns to me first. "I should have you arrested for kidnapping her," he hisses to me once the assistant leaves and seals us into privacy. He looks over at Gregory next. "And I fired you. What the hell are you doing here?"

"Daddy, stop," Alexis says. "Danny didn't kidnap me. I asked *him* to run away with *me*. And as for Gregory, I hired him, and you know what? He's one of the few people I can actually trust." She turns to Gregory. "You are *not* fired. You're very much still the head of my security team."

He ignores her and looks at me again. "What the fuck have you done to my daughter?"

I press my lips together, refusing to back down from this man. "I fell in love."

"Love? *Love*? That's nice. Now get out." His command is firm.

"He's not going anywhere," Alexis says softly, linking her arm through mine at the elbow and hugging mine to her chest. "He's here to stay because I fell in love with him, too."

I think she's about to expand on that with exactly where our love led us when her father roars at us. "Where the hell have you been? You ran out on the wedding, and I've been working nonstop to fight off the media and their thousands of questions while chasing you down for the last nine days!"

"We didn't want to be found. We needed time," she says softly.

"You don't get time!" he yells. "You don't get to make those decisions!"

"So I was just supposed to marry Brooks because you told me to?" she presses, and I'm not sure she should be poking an angry bear, but the words are out.

"Yes. That's *exactly* what you were supposed to do." His volume is lower, but the threat is still behind his words.

She shakes her head. "You don't control me. I will not allow it a second longer." Her arms are still wrapped around one of mine, and she's squeezing so hard I'm fairly certain I'm losing circulation, but I deal with it. I'm here to hold her up however I can.

"You don't have a choice, little girl," he hisses.

"I'm not a little girl anymore, and it's high time I take control of my life," she shoots back.

"You signed that control away," he reminds her.

"When I was sixteen. Sixteen! Don't you get that? I'm two years from thirty, and you're still acting like I'm a child!"

We all hear a soft knock at the door interrupting the incredibly tense moment between father and daughter while the three other men in the room watch the spectacle unfolding before us.

Gregory glances around the room before he heads over to open it.

"Ms. Bodega, we need you backstage for some lighting tests," another assistant tells us.

Alexis nods. "Yes, of course." She's composed as always despite the fight with her father when she turns to look at me. "You're okay?"

"I'm fine," I say softly.

She looks into my eyes a few more beats, and then she nods before she turns to follow the assistant out of the room.

When the door closes and I'm left alone with these three men, my chest tightens. At least I know Gregory is on my side, but they don't trust him.

I can't be the one to tell her father that we're married now, but the rings on our left hands didn't do us any favors to hide that fact. We're not hiding it, anyway. But I'm sure she'd want to be here for that particular announcement.

"I'll ask you again, boy," her father hisses at me. "What have you done to my girl?"

Well, aside from the fact that she's *my girl* now…

I don't lead with that.

"I told you, sir. I simply fell in love with her."

He shakes his head. "That's not good enough." He takes a step toward me as if he's going to intimidate me into relenting, but he's an older man who's still recovering from two recent bouts with pneumonia. Healthy or not, he's no match for a professional athlete.

I stand my ground firmly.

"I will ruin you, Mr. Brewer. Do you understand me?" he threatens. "I will ruin you and your family and everything dear to you if you carry on with this charade."

"Leave my family the fuck out of this. It's between Alexis and me, and I will not stand here listening to your threats when I'm here to support Alexis." I spin on my heel with those words and exit the little room, beelining for the stage to be with my girl instead of listening to her father's empty threats for another second.

At least…I *hope* they're just empty threats.

Chapter 2
Alexis

I'm standing on my spot as the light finds me, and I'm worried.

I'm more than worried.

I'm a wreck.

My stomach is in knots, and it has nothing to do with the fact that I'm about to sing for a large crowd gathered here in this amphitheater as we broadcast to live television.

None of that worries me in the least.

My dad is alone with Danny. We haven't told him we're married.

He's not going to take the news well.

How can I give a good performance tonight when I have no idea what's happening in that room?

He blames Danny for all of this when I haven't had the chance to explain any of it…which I guess lies on myself since I'm the one who chose to run away.

He knew I didn't want to marry Brooks, and he didn't care. He wouldn't have listened to any sort of explanation I had, so he pushed me into a corner. And when a person is backed into a corner, sometimes they act out of fear.

A small part of me wonders whether I married Danny out of fear. After all, we rushed it ahead a couple of days just to ensure if my father *did* find us, he couldn't make me marry Brooks.

But a bigger part of me knows the truth. I married him because I fell in love with him. It was inevitable that we'd end up here, and the way it all went down was perfect for us.

It wasn't the fanfare that my father wanted. It was small—tiny, really—and intimate. It was just for us. No helicopters flying overhead. No paparazzi waiting outside. It was last-minute, and the circle of people who knew was limited, which gave us exactly the wedding we wanted.

Will we celebrate sometime down the road with a huge party?

Maybe.

Is that what we need?

Definitely not.

I'm happy with how it all went down, and to be perfectly honest with myself, I'm glad my father wasn't there. Clearly the institution of marriage means nothing to him if he had the gall to force me into wedded bliss with Brooks, so I think it's better that the true marriage I want for myself began without him there.

But as soon as this performance is over, I know I'll have questions for him, too.

I don't want Brooks in the room when I ask the question that's really on my mind. *Why did you want me to marry Brooks so badly?*

I'll study him carefully to see whether he admits the truth or fabricates yet another lie.

Because at this point, it feels like a whole lot of lies piled on top of one another. And I can't wait to get to the truth…and to *tell* him my truth, too.

I run through my scales and warm-ups, and the same assistant who led me out here brings me a cup of tea while I stand on my mark. I hand the empty cup back when I have thirty seconds left to go.

I draw in a deep breath. This is my first performance as a married woman, and I'm not sure why that pulses an excitement deep inside me.

The curtain opens, and I'm the first performer.

I hear my name, and the crowd erupts into applause as I smile and wave.

"O holy night," I begin, and this isn't a song to play around with. I dig deep, putting everything I have into the song, and it still feels like somehow it's not enough.

Probably because I'm worried.

Is Danny still in that room with my father and Brooks? What are they saying to him? Are they brainwashing him to think or act a certain way?

He's too strong. He won't give in. We both know this is right.

But how can I perform here when I'm worried about what's going on there?

I'm about to start the second verse when my eyes drift to the side of the stage, and there I see Danny watching me.

He's mouthing the words along with me, and he's watching me with…

Gratitude. Warmth. Adoration.

Love.

My chest seems to open up a little, and I dig even deeper to belt out the next verse.

Just making eye contact with him was enough to push me to go where I've never gone before as relief pulses through me.

He is everything to me.

If I had to give all this up just for another moment where my hand clutches his, I'd do it in a heartbeat.

If my father threatens my career, he can have it if it means I can have Danny.

If my father threatens to hold onto my masters, they're his forever if I get another day with the man I love.

I don't care about any of it because it's all meaningless unless I have him.

I slide right into "Silent Night" next, and another singer, Ivy Wilson, joins me on stage for the second verse. For the third, country singer Mandy Davis joins in. The crowd gathered here erupts in huge applause at the end of the song, and we wave our thanks as the live program cuts to commercial.

I rush to the side of the stage. "I'm so glad you're here. What did he say?"

He shakes his head. "This is about you right now. What can I get you?"

I stare at him for a beat.

That's *never* been anybody's answer to me.

I'm here singing. It's my job. I put aside my personal stuff to perform the way I'm expected to perform.

Perhaps that's the greatest acting job of all.

"God, I love you," I murmur, and I press a kiss to his cheek that's surely captured by *somebody* in the audience.

I hope it was. I hope people can see the love I have for this man.

If they don't, they will soon since my next album is going to have him all over it.

Chapter 3
Alexis

The performance goes well after that. I feel at home on this stage only because he's there for me, making sure I'm comfortable and cared for, and it's more than I can say for my father or Brooks, who are likely still in that room yelling at Gregory.

They don't know about Gregory's hand in helping me—or maybe they do and that's why my father so badly wanted to fire him.

I dread the end of this gig if only because now I'm going to have to really face the music as my father waits back there for the answers I have yet to give him.

It's been nice being in this dream world for the last nine days, but my time is obviously up.

"That was incredible, Lex," Danny murmurs into my hair after the show ends as I walk off the stage and straight into his arms. "*You* are incredible. That was…Jesus. I don't even have words. Your talent is so fucking raw, and listening to you sing those songs was just…" He shakes his head a little, clearly at a loss. "It was fantastic. Stunning. Every second of it."

I'm much taller with the extra six inch heels, but he still towers over me. He bends down and presses his lips to mine, and I don't know if I've ever felt more cared for in my entire life.

He's here.

My dad isn't.

Brooks isn't.

But it's time to face them.

I grab Danny's hand as we make our way back to the dressing room.

Sure enough, my father is sitting on the couch and Brooks is perched in a chair. Gregory is nowhere to be found.

"Where's Gregory?" I demand as I walk into the room.

My father stands, and his eyes meet mine. He hasn't gotten any less angry since I left the room over two hours ago. "He's been excused for the evening."

"You have no right or authority to do that." I snarl a little at him as I say the words.

"If you'll excuse us, I need to talk to my daughter," he says to Danny.

I clutch him more tightly to me. "He stays."

He purses his lips a beat, and then he grits out between a clenched jaw, "Fine." He heaves in a heavy breath. "Let's start at the beginning then, shall we?"

I clear my throat. "Let's start with how this Christmas special just went. Are you really not going to say a word about it? Oh, right. Because you sat in here and waited for it to end instead of watching me and supporting me from the side of the stage the way Danny did for me."

"Is that what this is about? You want me to baby you after twelve years in the business? Are you kidding me right now?" my father demands. He doesn't wait for a response. "Tell me why you ran out on the wedding."

"Because I love Danny and I couldn't marry someone else I don't love. It's really as simple as that." I fold my arms across my chest.

"You have fucked everything up," my father says, and suddenly I see a desperation in his eyes that I hadn't noticed before.

Meanwhile, Brooks sits silently in the chair scrolling his laptop, almost as if he isn't paying any attention to this scene at all.

Maybe he isn't.

Or maybe there's something else going on here that I can't even begin to understand.

"What have I fucked up?" I ask, throwing his own words back at him, which makes him flinch. "The wedding to Brooks? Okay, you're right. I did mess that one up pretty good. But asking me to do it at all was pretty messed up, too."

"You have a contract to abide by," he reminds me.

"No." I shake my head, my word calm and simple in the quiet room.

"What do you mean *no*?" he shouts at me.

"I mean…*no.* I'm an adult who is capable of making my own decisions." I stand firmly at my words.

"I've given you freedom and liberties you don't even realize, my dear. And if that's the ground you're going to take, we go to the contract."

"I'm sorry, Dad, but nowhere in the contract does it say I have to marry who you say I have to marry. I may not have memorized every detail, but of that I am certain." I purse my lips as I await his reply.

"The contract says you do not in fact have any such power to make decisions that affect your career without first consulting with your agent."

"Who I marry has nothing to do with my career. Or it didn't, until you made it that way with Brooks," I argue.

Danny slides in beside me, standing close enough that I can feel him without him actually touching me.

"I married Danny," I whisper, and my dad's head whips to mine as his eyes light on fire.

Brooks lifts to a stand but remains silent.

"You *what*?" my father demands.

"I married Danny," I repeat. I hold up my ring finger with the gorgeous infinity band on it and his name tattooed along the side.

My father's jaw drops, and there's something deeply satisfying about shocking him in this way. "You will get it annulled."

"No, I will not." I slide my arm around Danny, and he throws his arm around my shoulder, drawing me close into his side.

"Then I will ruin him and everything dear to him," my father says.

"I love your daughter very much, sir, and I will do whatever I can to support her and her brand, which I know is incredibly important to her. But I will not stand by and take your threats," Danny says, his voice firm in this small room, and I don't know if I've ever loved him more.

I tighten my arm around him in solidarity.

My father stares between the two of us for a few beats. "You'll both live to regret this. I guarantee you that."

He takes those words and storms out of the room. Brooks gives me some sort of look that I can't quite decode.

My eyes meet Danny's.

I don't know what's coming next, but I do know that at least I'll have this man by my side through it all.

Chapter 4
Danny

Well…now what?

Her dad just stormed out after threatening me and my family, so that's something. Brooks is still standing in this small room with us keeping things as awkward as possible, so I turn to him.

"What do you get out of all of this?" I ask him. "Why did you go along with the wedding?"

His brow furrows as he keeps a mighty strong poker face. "I wanted to marry the woman I love."

"Pfft," Alexis scoffs.

He gives her a long gaze before he walks out of the room.

"It's a lie," she says. "Plain and simple. He does not love me. We talked about how this is nothing more than a business deal. I'm not even sure he knows what love is unless we're talking about money."

Money.

Her words give me a clue as to what's really behind all of this, but I'm not going to say anything until I dig a little…until I get to the truth. I don't want to give her any more anxiety than she's already dealing with over all this, anyway.

But I do have one question, and that's…what comes next? The hard part is over—the part where we told her father that we're married now. We have no idea what the fallout will be, but I can't imagine she wants to go home and spend the night there and wake up on Christmas morning like everything's fine when it isn't.

"What do you want to do now?" I ask.

She shrugs. "I have no idea. I just know I don't want to go back to my father's house right now."

"What about Vegas?" I ask.

Her eyes meet mine. "Vegas? Like…your house?"

"Our house. For now, anyway. Until we buy something better."

"Oh," she murmurs, and I'm having a hard time getting a gauge on how she really feels about that. "Yes. I *love* Vegas. It's always felt like home, and now, with you…it'll *be* home. And it's not far from LA. Maybe we could get a place here, too, for when I have to work here."

"I love that idea," I say softly.

"I want to wake up on Christmas morning in your arms and that's all I need. Aside from bacon. And maybe donuts." She shrugs a little at the end.

"I'm down for all of that, but I have one request," I say, my eyes glinting as I pull her into my arms.

"Anything," she breathes as her eyes connect with mine.

"I want to unwrap you like the gift you are, and then I want to fuck you like the vixen you are."

Her eyes widen and her breathing hitches at my words.

Oh, it's going to be a merry Christmas indeed.

I text Gregory and ask him how we can get our stuff here and how we can get to Vegas tonight, and he lets me know that he already has it in the back of the car waiting for us behind the amphitheater and I'm welcome to drive that to Vegas or we can see if there's a red-eye flight available.

We head that direction, and he ushers us safely toward the Yukon waiting for us. There's nobody back here—we're underground, and it's safe and deserted since most everybody has already cleared out.

We don't get in the vehicle yet as Alexis moves to say goodbye to Gregory.

"I just wanted to have a quick word with you," he says, his eyes on Alexis.

"What is it?"

"First, here's this," he says, handing over her phone. "Second, I wanted to tell you that your father is not taking the news well that you married Mr. Brewer." His tone is gentler than I think I've ever heard out of him.

"I didn't imagine he would," she mutters.

"No, but he's already actively looking into Danny's family for weaknesses. I will do whatever I can to protect them, but you know your father's connections. If he finds something he can use, he won't hesitate to weaponize it." His tone is less gentle with these words as his gaze shifts to me.

"My father," I whisper.

He nods. "Your father."

"He hasn't been in touch with me yet," I say.

Gregory's brow furrows. "He had to have noticed by now that he was hacked and all his data is gone."

"Unless…" I trail off as I think about the worst. What if he died and I don't even know?

"Yeah," Gregory grunts. "Unless. I'll see what I can find out."

"Thank you," I say, feeling suddenly very much like he's part of my family, too.

"Where will you go for Christmas?" Alexis asks him, moving toward him for a quick embrace.

One side of his mouth lifts up in what's *almost* a smirk. "I'll be fine."

She studies him a few extra beats, and then she nods. "Okay. Merry Christmas. Thank you for all you do for me."

He offers a genuine—albeit small—smile. "It's an honor, ma'am. Thank you for giving me some of the best years of my life."

They hug, and then we slip into the car and start the long drive toward home.

It's after two in the morning when we arrive back home. Alexis closed her eyes through most of it as we let the low hum of soft Christmas music fill the air.

And I thought about my father.

I really don't have a whole lot of memories from *before*—you know, when he was still a part of our family and lying to my mother while he broke his vows every time he slept with someone who wasn't my mother.

The majority of my memories of him come *after*.

Before it happened, the man was my hero. He could do no wrong. It's hard to look back and remember much about that time in my life. It feels like he hasn't been a hero in an awfully long time.

But what if it's true? What if the reason why he's been silent is because he's not around to speak anymore? Or what if he took a turn and he's in the hospital?

How would I feel if he really was dead?

It's not fair to say I'd be better off. I wouldn't wish that on anybody—even the man who is actively trying to ruin my life.

It's just not how I was raised—by my mother, anyway.

But would I be? If I didn't have him lurking in the background ready to strike, would I be better off?

Maybe. But maybe someone else would step into his shoes, and I don't doubt it given Alexis's astronomical fame. There will be people out there who hate me simply for existing. There will be people out there who wish horrible things upon me without knowing the first damn thing about me.

But that's on them. I won't contribute to the negative vibes when this world already has far too many of them floating around.

I guess that begs the question…if he *is* still living and breathing, what am I going to do about it?

If he's gone, what am I going to do about it?

For the longest time, I've felt like I only had one parent—my mother. Because I have. She's what a real parent *should* be. She's supportive and loving. She looks out for me. She protects me. She encourages me. She does whatever she can to help me.

And I wasn't always an easy kid. I made it out the other side okay, but I was a bit of a rebel back in my teenage years. I don't think I even thought about the idea of settling down at all until Alexis came into my life.

But my mother was always there for me regardless.

What would *she* want me to do when it comes to my father?

She wouldn't want me holding onto the negativity. That's for sure.

She wouldn't want me hurting. She wouldn't want me anxious over it.

I don't know if she'd want me to forgive him, but it seems like she did a long time ago. Maybe not *forgive* so much as realize how very much better off she was without him in her life.

The time in the car passes quickly as I contemplate all of it, and ultimately, I have an inclination of what I want to do.

He didn't teach me to be the bigger man, but I want to be anyway.

If there's still time.

Chapter 5
Alexis

"Merry Christmas." His voice is soft and dreamy, and maybe I *am* dreaming, or maybe this is reality.

Maybe reality is a dream.

I'm waking up in my husband's arms, and if you would've told me *last* Christmas I'd be waking up as Danny Brewer's wife *this* Christmas, I wouldn't have believed it for a second.

Yet here we are.

"Merry Christmas," I murmur back, and I feel his cock near my ass as he pushes his hips toward me. I slept in a t-shirt and panties, and the thin fabric of his boxers against my panties is the only thing separating us. "I didn't get you anything."

"I've got something for you," he taunts, pushing his hips toward me again. "Spoiler alert. It's my cock."

I giggle, and I turn in his arms toward him. "That's the kind of gift I'd love to wake up to on Christmas morning."

"I told you I wanted to unwrap you, and then you fell asleep," he says, and he pouts a little.

"Everybody knows you have to wait for Christmas morning to unwrap your gift."

His eyes light up a little as a smile lifts one corner of his lips. Warmth spreads through me, landing square between my legs as the familiar ache pulses down low.

He traces a fingertip along my torso and down to my hip, and he slips a finger between my panties and my skin at my hip as he offers a soft moan.

Anticipation builds within me as I wait for his finger to lower down, but instead, he pulls his hand away, shifts, and moves over the top of me. He pulls my shirt over my head, and he slowly slides my panties down my legs. He moves up to press a soft kiss to my lips, and then he trails his lips to my neck, down to my breasts, where he stops to enjoy my nipple between his lips, and then down my torso to my stomach. He peppers soft kisses on his way, the hum of his moans telling me he's enjoying this gift as much as he loves the main event.

He kisses my hip where his finger was only moments ago, and then he moves over toward my pubic bone. He skips down a little lower, kissing the inside of my thigh, and then he pushes my legs apart. Instead of diving in like I want him to, like I *need* him to, he moves back up to my naval. He kisses me there, then trails back to my hip, teasing me when he knows what I want.

He glances up at me and shoots me a devilish grin, and the ache between my legs is searingly hot as I look at this man who has come to mean so much to me. His fingertips move to my hips, and he holds me down as he finally dips his head between my legs.

His tongue reaches out to my clit, and he flicks it there, sending a shockwave through my entire core. I moan as my hips move to jerk up off the bed, but he's holding me down.

"Mm," he murmurs. "So wet already." His breath is a cool breeze against my hot flesh.

He does it again with a little more pressure this time, and it's like he's pressing on the ache to make it bigger and stronger, this tangible thing in the room that I could cling onto with every pulse of his talented tongue.

My heart pounds as I wait for each new flick of his tongue, and I push my entire body down when his tongue connects the next time, the need for friction nearly unbearable as I cry out.

"Naughty girl," he warns, but then he dips his tongue into my pussy, and it's exactly the small measure of relief I needed.

He moves his tongue in and out as he continues to hold me down, and then he flicks it up again against my clit.

Oh my God.

I can't take it.

It's so good, so, so good, and so close, but it's too far away. He's moving too slowly, and I need him to push his cock into me and finish me off.

I need this release.

He must sense it because he lets go of my hips where he's holding me down, and I start to move along with him as he picks up the pace. He buries his face in my pussy, licking and sucking as I gyrate along with him, and then his lips move to my clit. He sucks there as he slides two fingers into my pussy, and I scream out with pleasure.

But then he adds a finger into my ass, and I'm done.

The feeling is too good, too full, too hot. I can't hold on even though I don't want this onslaught of pleasure ever to end.

His tongue flicks over my throbbing clit once more, and it's enough to send me over the cliff into a violent climax. I'm incoherent as I scream or moan or cry his name, and I thrash against his mouth as he continues his brutal attack of pleasure on me. I fist the sheets as I continue to tremble with pleasure, and he doesn't stop. He keeps delivering the sweet, vicious bliss until the quaking starts to slow and I'm left gasping for breath.

And when it's all over, I'm so sated and depleted that I can't even think straight. My heavy lids are half-closed as I watch him wipe his mouth with the back of his hand, and I can't help but think this might be the very best Christmas morning of my entire life.

He excuses himself to the restroom, and I think I fall back asleep for a few minutes. I wake with a jerk when the bed dips beside me, and I realize he hasn't gotten his own release just yet.

I want him to fuck me like he said he would, but I also want to taste him.

And since it's Christmas morning and we have all day together with no other plans, why not both?

I wait for him to lean back on his pillows with a soft sigh, and then I force myself up. I slowly pull his boxers down his legs, lifting them up over his incredibly hard cock, and I toss them aside. I kneel between his legs, and I get right to work.

I take his cock in my fist and stroke up and down a few times, and his eyes are heavy as he looks down at me, a small smile playing on his lips.

I look up at him and lick my own lips. "What?" I ask.

He reaches down and tucks some hair behind my ear. "Nothing. Just…I don't think there's anything more beautiful than you all flushed after you come, excited to take my cock between your lips."

His words alone send another aching pulse square to my pussy.

My God, this man.

"How do you know I'm excited?" I ask.

He sits up and reaches down between my legs. He pushes a finger into me. "Because you're so goddamn wet that you want more."

My hips sway to the movement of his finger, and I close my eyes.

He's right. He's so, so right.

But he deserves a turn first.

I shift my hips back so his finger falls out, and I suck his cock into my mouth as he lays back to enjoy what I'm doing.

He watches me, and I glance up to see his eyes on me. They're heated with need and lust and love and everything in between, and he reaches down to hold my head in place as I suck him all the way to the back of my throat. He relents, letting me pull back, and I suck in a breath as I do it again.

"Oh fuck," he groans, and then his hips start to shift so he's keeping pace with my mouth. His growls and groans tell me he's getting close. "I want to fuck you. I want to come in your hot cunt, baby."

I stop sucking on him and quickly move over the top of him, sliding my pussy down over the wet cock that was just in my mouth.

"Fuck," he groans, drawing out the word, and he lifts up a little so his face is inches from mine. "I love you," he says, and I wrap my arms around his shoulders as he clings on around my waist.

"I love you, too," I say, and then he buries his face in between my breasts as he starts to move the two of us from the bottom.

"Oh fuck, fuck, fuck!" he grunts, and hearing his pleasure as I feel the fullness of him inside of me is enough to push me into another orgasm.

As my pussy tightens and pulses over him, he lets out a loud roar and then pumps hard into me a few more times before his rhythm slows.

We're both panting and glistening with sweat as I lift myself off of him and collapse down beside him.

"That was one hell of a wakeup call," he murmurs.

I giggle as I lean up to look at him. "I'll take one of those every morning from now until forever."

"May your Christmas wish come true," he says, and he presses a soft kiss to my forehead.

And despite all the drama and turmoil surrounding us, I feel safe right here in his arms, in his bed, in this cocoon where we find ourselves.

I just wish we could stay here forever.

But eventually, reality will come knocking.

Chapter 6
Danny

I open the front door and find the box of food I ordered sitting there.

I felt bad ordering food delivery on Christmas morning, so I tipped well. I wasn't sure how else to get bacon and fresh donuts here as a surprise. I don't have much else for her to open and I haven't even been home for the last nearly two weeks to fill the house with fresh food.

"I have a surprise for you," I say, and I walk into the kitchen with the box of food, where I find her making us hot chocolate.

"What is it?" she asks, and her eyes light up with excitement as she sets the mug down on the counter.

I push the box over toward her, and she opens it. "Ah!" she yells. "Chocolate long johns with sprinkles and bacon? You're the best!" She runs around to my side of the counter and throws her arms around me. "Thank you!"

I drop a kiss to her lips. "Merry Christmas."

"This is everything I wanted."

"Donuts and bacon?" I ask. "You're easy to please."

She laughs as she shakes her head. "No. Donuts, bacon, and *you*."

I kiss her again, and then she scrambles out of my arms for the bacon.

"I see where I fall in your list of priorities," I say, folding my arms.

"We already did it once this morning. I need some fuel for more of that later."

I chuckle. "Deal."

We eat breakfast, and once she's done licking the chocolate off her fingers, which awakens my cock again, I shift in my seat and say, "I have one more Christmas gift for you."

She narrows her eyes at me. "I have one for you, too."

"I thought you said you didn't have anything for me," I say.

"I *did* say that, but as it happens, I seem to have found one. Or, rather, Gregory helped me out with mine."

"That's funny because my mom helped me out with mine," I say.

"You go first," she says.

I nod. "Okay." I run upstairs and grab the piece of paper I printed late last night after she had already fallen asleep, and I put it into a little gift bag I found on my closet shelf.

I bring it down and find her still standing by the counter. I hand the bag to her.

She narrows her eyes at me, and then she opens the bag, pulls out the paper, and starts reading it before her eyes fall on the photo.

Her eyes lift to mine. "Is this…"

"A house. For us. Here in Vegas. Much more private than this one, and a lot bigger. Ten thousand square feet, a gated neighborhood, a pool. Views of the Strip. Seven beds, nine baths. Beautiful palm trees all over the backyard and privacy bushes in the front. More deserving of Alexis Bodega, though

I'm not sure anything would ever really be grand enough for you."

"Alexis *Brewer*," she chastises, and I chuckle.

"Right. Caroline Alexis Brewer."

She starts to laugh a little.

"What? You don't like it?"

She shakes her head. "No, no. I *love* it." She slides her phone across the counter toward me, and she has a listing pulled up for a house. At second glance I realize…it's *our* house. Well, the rental—the one where we got married in San Diego. Her eyes light up when she says, "I had Gregory put in an offer. They accepted."

"It was for sale?" I ask.

She shakes her head. "We offered well over the estimated price for the place where I got to marry the man of my dreams. Now we'll have a place close to your mom right on the beach. I thought about checking into the one in Carmel, too, but I didn't want to invest in one so far north when we could just go back and visit anytime we want." She's babbling a little, likely nervous about the gift for me just as I was about the gift for her.

I grab her into my arms. "So we bought each other…*houses* for Christmas?" I ask.

"I think we did, hubby." She giggles, and I press a kiss to her lips.

The future is sure looking blindingly bright for us despite the threats lurking in the background.

Still, there's something missing from this celebration, and I can't help but think it's *family*. My mom, my sister. My nephews. I can't help but wonder whether Rush proposed, whether he's there this morning with her and the boys. What Santa brought them for Christmas. If they're eating cinnamon rolls and drinking hot chocolate with candy canes in them like we used to do every Christmas morning.

I can't help but wonder if my mom is there, and for some reason, I wonder where Gregory is, too.

I've been so wrapped up in being there for Alexis that I abandoned my own family.

But I also can't help but feel a little sadness from Alexis. Her father has always been an important part of not just her career, but her entire life. And he's missing from it now.

I don't know if they've ever spent Christmas apart. They were once so close, and around the same time that I stepped into her life, they started growing apart.

It's coincidental timing. She was looking for an out, and she found it in me.

But I suppose I get why her father would blame me. I get why he'd want me out of the picture. Still, if we can find a way to work together instead of against each other, I feel like we'd be able to conquer the entire world.

So my silent gift to my wife is my secret vow to myself.

I am going to win over her father—and not just because he's threatening my family and my own livelihood.

I'll win him over so I can help patch up his relationship with his daughter.

I just have to figure out how exactly I'm going to do that.

Chapter 7
Alexis

After breakfast, Danny asks if we can video chat with his sister, and of course I agree. She answers right away as we settle in beside each other on Danny's couch.

"Merry Christmas!" She's wearing festive Christmas pajamas and a Santa hat, and she flips the video to show the boys playing with new toys in a heap of wrapping paper under the tree.

I spot Rush sitting on the couch watching the boys fondly, and my heart feels so happy that Anna has found some happiness with him. I got to know him a little better when we were in San Diego, and since he and Danny are so close, I feel like I'll get to know him more and more as time goes on.

"Merry Christmas!" Danny says. "Hey Lucas and Leo, was Santa good to you?"

"Yes!" both boys yell back at the same time, and Danny chuckles.

"Thanks to their uncle," Anna mutters, and I can't help but wonder what that means. Is Danny one of Santa's elves?

It wouldn't surprise me. He loves his family and when he loves, he loves hard.

"Is that Rush Ross I see sitting on your couch?" Danny asks.

"In fact, it is, and guess what?" Anna says excitedly.

"What?" we ask at the same time.

"We're engaged! Ahh!" She holds her hand in front of the phone to show us the big rock gracing her ring finger.

"Whoa! Congratulations!" Danny says.

"You knew, didn't you," she accuses, and Danny makes a sarcastic face that says *nope, no way, sure didn't.*

We chat a few more minutes as Anna tells us how they're going to wait a while before tying the knot, but they're moving to Vegas before the kids go back to school after winter break—which means in the next two weeks. "We found a place, and it's a quick close."

"We're moving, too," Danny says. "I put in an offer on a place up near Spring Valley, and they accepted."

"That's where we're going, too!" Anna says.

Anna and I both squeal as we think about how close we'll be. I finally have the kind of sister I always wanted.

"Is Mom there?" Danny asks Anna, and she shakes her head.

"She was very mysterious about her plans, but she said she'd be by in the afternoon." She shrugs.

"I'll video chat her next and get to the bottom of things," Danny says, and Anna laughs.

"Good luck with that." Leo and Lucas start arguing over one of the toys, and Anna says, "Gotta run. Love you guys." She ends the call, and we glance at each other.

"Wow," I breathe. "Rush Ross is going to be my brother-in-law."

"Keep it in your pants, woman." He rolls his eyes, and I giggle.

He dials his mom next, and when she answers, she's smiling. "Merry Christmas!"

"Merry Christmas, Mom," he says warmly. "What are you up to?"

She clears her throat, and she's looking away from the screen and giving a *look*. It's that mom look where she's widening her eyes and furrowing her brow at the same time with disapproval.

"Who are you looking at?" Danny asks.

"Nobody," she says, and she does it again as she gives the same look to whoever she's with.

Clearly whoever is with her wants to be in the chat, and she doesn't want it.

"What's going on?" Danny presses.

"Nothing. Why do you ask?" Her voice is a little higher than usual, which gives her away immediately. She clears her throat and looks away. "I'm just hanging out here at home all alone, getting ready to go to Anna's in a bit."

"All alone? Prove it," Danny says.

"I don't have to prove a thing to you. Now tell me, how are you two today?" she asks, trying but failing to shift the subject off herself.

Danny narrows his eyes at his mother. "Fine."

"Did you exchange gifts?" she asks.

"Mm-hm," Danny murmurs.

"And how did you each like the houses?" She freezes for a beat, and then she gasps. "Oh!" She slaps a hand over her mouth.

"Wait a minute. How'd you know what she got for me?" Danny asks, onto her little fib now.

"Oh, fine. You know I can't lie worth a darn anyway." She moves to the other side of the room, and there stands Gregory beside her.

Smiling.

Smiling.

I've never seen the man smile a day in his life, but Danny's mom clearly makes him happy.

"Merry Christmas, Gregory," I say with a wide smile of my own.

"Thank you, ma'am."

"Oh, stop with that nonsense today," I chide. "What's going on here?"

"Well, Gregory and I got to working together to make sure you two were safe and protected, and we sort of just…well…I guess we just kind of…"

"Bonded," Gregory fills in for her.

"Yes. We bonded," she says.

"Bonded?" Danny repeats. "As in…"

"Oh, stop it, Danny!" his mom says, her cheeks turning bright red as she giggles like a schoolgirl.

I nudge him in the ribs with my elbow, and he chuckles.

"Well we won't keep you if you have more, uh…*bonding* to do." Danny gives me a look, and I giggle.

"No! We're all done bonding for today!" his mother assures us, and my giggle turns into a full-on laugh. "We need to get over to Anna's. Bye!" She ends the call, and Danny turns to look at me.

"Well," he says, clearly at a loss for words.

"I mean, I kind of suspected," I admit.

"Yeah. I did, too, but to see the evidence right in front of my face…"

"It's nice," I say. "I'm happy for them. He's the best, Danny. Really. And your mom, she's a sweetheart. They're a good match."

"But he won't be around for her when he's traveling with you," he points out.

"Just like I won't be around for you when I'm traveling with him." I press my lips together as the sad reality plows into us a little harder than either of us was expecting.

He reaches his arm around me, and I lean into his chest.

"We'll deal with it as it comes," he says softly.

I nod, and we put on some Christmas movies and settle in to enjoy each other's company for the rest of the day, warm and cozy under a blanket as we snuggle.

I already know we're building memories I'll be able to hold onto when we're apart. That time is coming, and it's a sad reality we're going to have to face sooner than later.

Chapter 8
Alexis

I wait all day to hear from my father, but a call never comes.

A text never comes.

Nothing.

I finally text him just after dinner.

Me: Merry Christmas, Dad. I'm sorry we didn't get to spend time together today. I hope you can understand why I did what I did.

By the time I drift off to sleep, I still haven't heard from him.

And I'm not quite sure how to take that. Is he just shutting me out because he's mad? Or is he planning something?

I feel a little sad about it, but I'm not going to let it ruin my day. I'm sure he has plans for other ways to ruin my day, anyway.

When I wake in the morning, I have a text from Gregory waiting for me.

Gregory: We've run into a wrinkle with the house purchase. Call me when you can.

I slip out of bed where Danny's still sleeping and pull on one of his sweatshirts. It's huge on me, and it's warm and cozy, and it smells like Danny.

It's mine now, obviously.

I slip downstairs and dial Gregory once I'm settled on the couch under a blanket.

"Ma'am," he answers.

"What's going on?" I ask.

"I got word that you don't have the funds to purchase the house in Mission Beach first thing this morning."

"What?" I gasp.

"I think your father might have frozen your assets," he says.

Businesses were closed yesterday due to the holiday, obviously, so that's why we didn't hear anything before now.

"Seriously?" I mutter. I knew full well he'd find a way to ruin my day, and this is a pretty damn good start. "Okay. We'll head back to Los Angeles. Clearly this is something I'm going to have to deal with in person."

"I'm not sure when he froze them," he adds. "You've been off the radar for some time now, so he may have done it when you first ran out on the wedding."

"Good call. I bet he did it thinking I wouldn't get far without them."

"Most likely. I'm still in San Diego but would be happy to meet you at Mr. Bodega's house," he says.

"Do you have anything at the house that you need?" I ask.

"Nothing I can't live without."

"Then I'm fine," I say. "You enjoy your time off with Tracy, okay? I'll need you next week when we're back to filming."

"Of course, ma'am."

He ends the call, and I'm heaving out a heavy sigh when Danny walks into the room.

"Who were you talking to, and what's wrong?" he asks, plopping down beside me. He yanks part of the blanket to cover his legs, too.

"Gregory said he thinks my father froze my assets and I can't pay for the house we put the offer on." I purse my lips as I lean my head back and stare up at the ceiling.

"What the fuck?" he mutters.

"I need to go to LA and confront him. And, you know, get everything I own out of the house since I don't want to live there anymore even if I can't afford to buy my own place." I roll my eyes. It sounds so ridiculous when I say it that way. I grossed over six hundred million on my last tour. Of course I can afford a twelve million dollar home on the beach.

His brows crinkle. "Then let's go."

My eyes meet his. "Let's go."

We're back on the road toward Los Angeles once again even though we've only been *home* for a day. At least Danny can check in with his mom and sister while we're in California, but I'm not exactly sure where we're going to stay since my dad's house feels less and less welcoming with every passing second.

I'm getting tired of the constant traveling. It's been my life for so long that I can't even remember a time when I just felt…stable.

"What are you thinking about?" Danny asks as we zoom down the highway.

"Just that all the travel is starting to wear on me. Back and forth to Los Angeles, Vegas, up and down California, and backwards to filming and the tour before that." I shrug. "It just feels constant, like I don't have a place to rest my head that's permanent, you know?"

"In my arms, baby," he says, and he reaches over to set his hand on my thigh.

"I know," I say, and I grab his hand in mine. "You are home to me now. You are. But I'm just starting to feel…unsettled. You know?"

"You *are* unsettled. You've hardly been in one place for more than a few nights at a time since…" he trails off as he waits for me to fill in the blank.

"Since I was sixteen," I admit.

"Jesus. At least I have three to four months at home after a season and traveling then is my choice."

"And here you are, stuck with me." I frown, and he turns his hand around to squeeze mine.

"Not stuck, Lex. It's my choice, like I said. I wouldn't be anywhere else than beside you."

I look over at him as love fills my chest. "I appreciate that. And I love what I do. I'm eternally grateful for the opportunities I've had because of this career. But sometimes…"

"You just want to run away from it all?" he guesses.

"I did run away from it all, and now I'm back, and I think that's the whole problem. I didn't outrun my problems. They were still waiting right here for me when we returned."

He huffs out a mirthless chuckle. "That's kind of the problem with problems, isn't it? They stand still unless we deal with them."

"You're very wise," I tease. "And thanks for coming with me to deal with this."

"You should know by now, Lex. I'd do anything for you." His voice is raspy and soft as he says the words, and I absolutely do know that by now.

"Right back at you, Brewer."

He smiles, and we head on toward Los Angeles to deal with our problems.

I wish I could say once and for all…but I have this gut instinct that this whole thing is going to get really complicated really quickly.

Chapter 9
Danny

In every comfortable patch of silence that falls over the front seat while we head toward Los Angeles, my brain works overtime.

I have to figure out some way to patch things up between her and her dad, but he's making it harder and harder.

Freezing her assets?

Seriously?

Who does that shit?

It's her money to spend, but he's had such a tight leash on her for her entire life, he's just yanking on the chain a little harder right now.

I can cover us. I don't have the kind of money she has, but I do all right for myself. Enough to purchase that house in Vegas. Maybe enough to snag the one in Mission Beach, too.

I don't care about the money, and I don't think she really does, either. We could live in a studio apartment with a futon and be happy as long as we're together.

But it's the principle of the thing. She earned that money, and he has no right at all to prevent her from doing whatever the fuck she wants with it.

Still, as we drive toward her father's house, time seems to slow down. The trip is a long drag, and it's probably because we just made this trip less than forty-eight hours ago in the opposite direction. Before that, we drove all over the long-ass state of California, covering close to five hundred miles between Carmel and San Diego and beyond that back up to Anaheim and to Los Angeles.

Jesus. I'm tired just thinking about it.

She's right—she hasn't really had a home base in a while now apart from when she's filming, and that's a grind, too. Early mornings and late nights, and time in Vegas when she was filming there.

She needs a home of her own. She deserves one. We both do, together. How else do we kick off our married life together if we can't *be* together?

That'll be the lifelong question given our careers. I'll be traveling a solid six months out of the year on top of spring training and the postseason, and she'll be traveling for tours. Who knows when we'll have this sort of time together again?

The grind of the season always weighs down on me come September, but then playoffs hit and that makes it all worth it—provided my team makes it into the playoffs.

But what about her? The grind of a tour weighs down on her, and then she gets home and immediately jumps into filming a movie. And not just any movie, but one where she believes she'll be a contender for a huge award, and then once that's done filming she's jumping right into recording her next album.

It's a lot.

And now her assets are frozen.

I feel for her, and I want to make it all better.

And that's why I'm planning to confront her father today. Alone.

I need to talk to him about the way he's treating her, and I need to help him see that I'm not the enemy here. I just want to support her in whatever way I can.

"Oh shit," she mutters as she scrolls her phone.

"What's wrong?" I ask, glancing over at her rather unusual use of a curse word. Her face is white as she reads an article.

"The paparazzi got wind of us. They're saying we snuck off and got married."

"Well…we did," I say, pointing out the obvious.

"Yeah, we did. But we're on our way to confront my father, and this isn't going to make things any easier," she says, turning off her phone and tossing it on the dashboard.

"No, you're right about that."

"The article dubbed you the bad boy of baseball and said that you're corrupting America's pop princess," she says softly.

"So you're saying they nailed it?" I tease.

She narrows her eyes at me. "This isn't the time for jokes."

"I'm sorry," I say immediately.

She sighs.

"Listen. You're *my* princess now, okay? And I will do whatever it takes to protect you from all of it."

She presses her lips together, and then she turns her gaze out the window.

"Hey, it'll be okay," I say softly.

"I know. I just know how important branding is to my father, and I know it's a big reason why he wanted me to marry Brooks. So this…this is going to be a big obstacle in our way as we try to win him over to our side."

"I'd like to talk to him when we get there. Alone." My voice is firm, but I try to go for some warmth in there, too.

"I don't think that's a good idea."

"I know. It's a terrible idea. But I also think it's a necessity." I shrug.

"Okay. But first we go in together. Then I run upstairs to pack a few things…like my pillow. Okay?" she asks.

I nod. "Okay."

We pull into the circular driveway of her father's mansion a little after two o'clock in the afternoon, and she keys something into the keypad at the front door. Her father walks into the foyer as if he saw us pulling in.

"What are you doing here?" he demands.

"I'd like to know why you froze my assets," she begins, and I don't think that's exactly the right start.

"We're here to talk," I say quietly, trying to smooth things over. "Did you have a nice Christmas?"

"Jesus, like I want to shoot the shit with *you*." He looks at me distastefully, like he just ate something sour.

I shrug. "Look, I'm trying. Like it or not, I'm now your son-in-law, and I have a few things I'd like to talk to you about."

"I have nothing to say to you," he says, lifting his chin in defiance.

Alexis looks back and forth between us like she's watching a tennis match. "I have some things to say myself," she says. "Starting with…unfreeze my assets. Now."

He purses his lips but doesn't say a word, and that's when I know the truth.

I'm not sure how I know. I just have this really strong feeling that I do.

It's as if some quiet force is intervening and whispering what's really going on.

It's the look on his face that gives him completely away, maybe, or his refusal to address what she's saying.

He didn't freeze her assets.

He took her money.

I stare off with him, certain I want to put words to my hunch but also certain I don't want to do it in front of Alexis.

"Daddy, why are you doing this to me?" she begs as tears start to freefall down her cheeks. "I thought we were on the same team, and anyone can see how much I love Danny. I never wanted to be with Brooks. Can't you see that? He wasn't right for me. Danny is. He takes care of me. He *loves* me. I know you loved Mom. I know you know what that feels like. Why wouldn't you want that for me, too?"

His eyes soften as he looks upon his crying daughter.

I watch him carefully to see whether he gives anything away. He's doing a good job of hiding it, but he doesn't quite have the acting chops his daughter does.

"Has money really driven this big of a wedge between us?" she asks, crying in earnest now. "The fame? Or is it the *power* you're after by merging with D-Three? I just…I don't get it. You fired Gregory, you're pushing me away, and yet you're keeping Brooks in here like he's untouchable. Why? Why, Daddy?"

He blows out a heavy breath, and he closes his eyes for a beat. "I'm only trying to provide the best path to the future you've asked me for." He sounds tired. Worn down. Fatigued. As if he's repeating the same thing for the hundredth time to a child who keeps asking the same question over and over.

Only Alexis isn't a child. She's an adult who deserves answers.

She's an adult who needs to figure out how to untangle her career from this conman.

More thoughts I can't put voice to—at least not in this crowd.

"I don't care about the awards anymore," she says, and her father steps back as if he's been physically struck by her words. "I've realized something over the last couple of weeks, and it's that the Grammy and Academy Award in the same year was *your* goal for me. It was never *my* goal for me, but you put it in my head and dug it in so hard that you made me think it was my own idea. I'll try my hardest to earn them. It's a rare and amazing accomplishment. But I'm knocking on thirty's door, and I'm still being treated like a teenager. What about what I want? What about my own dreams and goals…not the ones you've chosen for me?"

"What do you want, Alexis?" he asks, his posture rigid and his tone unforgiving.

She shakes her head as she shrugs a little, and then she holds both hands out in front of her, indicating me. "Love. Marriage. Home. Babies. Permanence." She looks over at me. "With him."

It's all the things we've talked about—or talked around, anyway—and it's all the things I want, too.

With her.

"And that's what I'm going to do whether you like it or not," she says to her father. The words are akin to those of a spoiled teenager not getting her way, but this is a completely different context. These words are beautiful as they're spoken by this adult in front of me who is standing up and taking her life into her own hands for the first time ever.

She's taking control back. It's the control she always deserved to have. The control that was stripped from her when she didn't know any better than to sign it away when she was a teenager with a dream.

I reach over and squeeze her hand in solidarity.

The accolades and awards and performances have been incredible, but I don't know if I've ever been more proud of my wife.

Chapter 10
Danny

"There's a lot at play here, Alexis. But what you haven't considered is how hurtful it is that you married someone and told me after the fact. What you two did is immature and childish, only proving that I've been treating you the way you deserve to be treated your entire life." He shakes his head with disgust, and he stalks out of the room.

She stares after him, sighing as her gaze stays on his retreating back. "We shouldn't have come."

I wait until he's out of earshot. "We had to, Lex. We're here for answers, and we're not leaving until we have them. Let me go in there and give it a try."

She sighs, but she relents as she nods. "Fine. But be careful."

I huff out a chuckle. "I can take him."

She purses her lips at me and nods down the hallway. "He's likely in his study. Go down the long hallway, turn to your left, and it's the first room."

"Thanks." I drop my lips down to hers for a beat to give us both a little extra strength in this moment. "We've got this, okay?"

She nods, and then she heads toward the stairs so she can get her pillow and other personal effects from her bedroom, and I head in the direction he just walked.

I peek into some of the rooms on my way as I look for him, my chest tingling with nerves as I go. I'm about to confront my wife's father, which sounds scary. I'm not scared of him, exactly, but I still have to force one foot in front of the other.

I'd really rather be just about anywhere else other than here doing this right now.

But as I remind myself, I'm doing this for her.

She deserves answers. She deserves her money. She deserves the world, and this man stopped giving that to her long ago.

I intend to find out why.

I find him in a sprawling study. Bookcases line the walls, and a heavy executive desk sits in front of them. He's standing as he stares up at something on one of the bookcases—I think a framed photo on one of those shelves behind his desk.

I knock on the doorframe loudly both to interrupt his thoughts and to announce my arrival.

He whirls around at the sound, and he tosses a paper he's holding down onto his desk. "What do you want?" he snarls at me.

I step into the room and close the door behind me. I have some accusations I'm about to hurl at him, and I don't want Alexis to worry until she has a reason to. I don't know that she'd be able to hear us since I just watched her walk upstairs, but I'd rather be safe than sorry.

I don't want her to worry until I uncover the real truth behind whatever's going on here.

"I know you didn't freeze her assets, and I'm here to find out what you did with Alexis's money. Does it have something to do with why you were trying to force the merger?" I demand as I walk a little closer to him.

"I don't know what you're talking about," he scoffs, and he takes a step toward me—almost defensively and almost like he's trying to keep me away from his desk. "All I know is that you are ruining her and her brand with your *bad boy of baseball* bullshit."

"Why are you doing this, Mr. Bodega?" I ask. I never thought I'd have a father-in-law, and either way, I'm not real formal with most adults. Still, this feels like the type of situation that warrants the title.

I try to get a view of the paper he set down, but I can't see it from here.

He lets out a heavy sigh. "We had it all lined up, and then you had to come in and fuck it up." He takes a menacing step toward me that really isn't nearly as menacing as he thinks it is, and I take a step toward him, too—mostly so I can get a look at the paper. I'm not sure why, but my gut is telling me there's something on it that I need to see. Maybe because of his reaction when I walked into the room. He threw it down on the desk like it was on fire.

His eyes fall to my ring finger, and I flex my fingers a little at the feel of his eyes on it.

"It was all set," he mutters, almost as if he's talking to himself and not me. "We were so close. All she had to do was walk down the aisle, and then *you* ruined it all." His eyes are angry venom as they flick to mine and back to my ring. "You don't deserve to be wearing that ring."

He ambles toward me, closing the gap between us, and he reaches for my ring finger. He lunges for my finger as if he's going to pull the ring off, and I shift away from him out of pure instinct to protect my hands at all costs.

He lunges at me again, and this time he trips into me, knocking me down to the ground as he attempts to grab my hand. I tear my hand away from him and it ends up on the ground first, breaking my fall as he crashes down on top of me, the two of us landing on the floor with a thud…my wrist bearing the brunt of the weight.

A throbbing, severe pain rockets through me as a snapping sound fills the quiet room. Maybe it doesn't—maybe it's just in my own head—but I definitely hear it, and I definitely feel it.

I gasp in agony.

He rolls off of me, and I sit up and move my left hand in front of my face, already knowing exactly what happened.

My eyes shift down to my wrist, which is hanging at an odd angle as the sharp, searing pain registers in my brain.

I already know it's broken.

The pain is intense.

It's not the first broken bone I've had in my life. Fingers, my ankle, my nose.

But this is my wrist.

I need this wrist to catch. I play first base. Every position is important, but anywhere from eighteen to twenty-one percent of plays are made at first.

I need this wrist to bat. I need it to stand at home plate, usually third in the batting order since I'm a power hitter, with the bat perched over my right shoulder, feet apart and knees bent as I wait for the ball to come firing at me.

This injury is going to set me back weeks. Maybe months.

We're at the end of December. I report for training camp two months from today. Opening day for our regular season starts in three months.

I don't *have* months to nurse an injury back to health.

But I don't have any choice. My wrist is broken.

I can only pray there's no nerve damage. I can only hope it's just a clean break.

But either way, this wouldn't have happened if not for the man sitting beside me on the floor. The same man who doesn't even realize what he just did to me. He doesn't realize my wrist is broken and it's because of him.

My father-in-law.

"What have you done?"

Chapter 11
Alexis

I squeeze my pillow to my chest.

This doesn't feel like home anymore. Maybe it never did. It was always my dad's home, and I never should've agreed to stay under his roof.

It made sense, though. I'm always traveling, so why have my own house that I'll never be at?

So I stayed. It was as much of a home as I could have even if it never felt quite right.

But there are still a few things I want to bring with me back to Vegas to my *new* home. My real home. The home I'll be sharing with my husband. I have to be back here January second to get back to filming, but that gives me another week where I can hole up with Danny, watch Christmas movies, have a honeymoon staycation, and eat bacon.

Okay, maybe not eat bacon *all* those days since, you know, cholesterol.

But most of the days.

And in the meantime, I can help him pack up his house so we can move into the new one in Vegas, and I'd like a house here in Los Angeles since I do spend a lot of time here. I don't care if it's a house in LA or Beverly Hills, or a condo in a high rise, or something on the beach near Malibu. And that house in San Diego. I still want that one.

All I really need is Danny.

But I won't have him once the season gets underway.

I pull a suitcase from the corner of my closet and start filling it with some of my favorite things, hopeful that Danny can work out whatever's going on with my dad.

I trust him to fix this for me.

I wouldn't have sent him into the lion's den if I didn't.

I work quickly since I want to get down to see what's going on with Danny and my dad, tossing the things I want into a suitcase. The framed photo of my mom and me when I was a kid. My pillow. A soft blanket with butterflies all over it that I've had for eighteen years—one of the last Christmas gifts my mom ever gave me. Some clothes and underwear from my dresser drawers along with my favorite comfy socks. Make-up and hair essentials.

I walk to my closet to get my favorite slippers, one of the comforts of home, and I stand in there for a few beats looking around.

Plush carpet lines the floors, and an ostentatious crystal chandelier hangs in the middle of the room over an island with plenty of drawers. My eyes roam over the shoes in between the framed album covers and the racks of dresses. A vanity sits on the far end, luxurious couches adorn one wall, and it's all so…

Useless.

It used to be my favorite room, and I think it's because it's the room where I could escape to. I'd lock the door and sit on the floor or the couch and just have a moment to myself.

I can't count how many times I did deep breathing exercises on the couch.

I can't imagine how often I sat in here daydreaming I'd be able to escape all this.

And now…I have.

Sort of.

I'm still held to tight reins, but I've taken the first step to gain my control back. I'll miss this room, but I won't miss feeling like a prisoner in my own home. I won't miss my father taking away my decision-making skills. I won't miss escaping to one room where I feel like I can actually be myself for a change.

I won't miss not being able to be whoever the hell I want to be instead of whatever brand he decided to create.

Maybe my brand shifts to something new. Women empowerment. Being in control of your own life.

I like the sound of that.

The things I've written for the next album run through my mind. They're mostly sweet and dreamy folksy ballads or pop hits like always, but maybe I want something else, something…more.

Rock. Electronic.

It's something to consider as I shift my brand in a new direction and show the world I'm not the sweet little princess they've painted me into being. I'm a woman. I'm a badass. I'm in fucking control.

I draw in a deep breath as I let that idea wash over me, and I pull a notepad out of the top drawer of the island.

I settle onto the couch for a beat and scribble down a few ideas, and then I toss the notebook into my suitcase with the rest of the stuff I'm taking with me.

And that's it. I zip it all tightly into a single suitcase—except the pillow and blanket, which are too big to fit. The rest of the stuff in here is meaningless and useless.

We'll buy what we need as I make plans for the future.

And the more I think about it…the more I'm starting to realize what direction I want my career to take next.

I drag my suitcase down the stairs and set it by the front door, and then I take a few steps down the hallway toward my dad's study.

It's quiet, so that's good. At least they aren't shouting at each other, which is sort of what I was expecting.

I pause outside the door as I listen for voices, and it's quiet in there.

But then I hear Danny.

"What have you done?" His voice is a loud bark, and the fury in his tone is what drives me to open the door.

"What's going o—" I start, but I cut myself short when I look at the scene before me.

Danny, sitting on the floor, his left wrist looking slightly deformed as he cradles it in his right hand.

My father, a few feet away, a hard look in his eyes as he shifts them away from my husband to me.

"Oh my God," I murmur, my eyes on Danny as I rush over and sink down to the floor beside him. "Can you move your fingers?"

He wiggles his fingers and winces.

"Can you make a fist?" I ask.

He shakes his head.

"We need to get you to an urgent care. Now," I say. I stand and face off against my father. "What happened?"

He doesn't shrink back despite the way I'm hissing at him. "It was an accident." His voice is flat. It's not defensive, though maybe it should be, and it's not apologetic. It's devoid of any emotion at all, and I guess I just never thought my father would stoop so low.

I look back at Danny with my brows raised, and he nods as if to confirm that detail.

I don't know the details, but I do know that with any injury, the sooner you get help, the better. And his wrist looks all wrong. He needs that wrist to play ball, and right now…he can't even make a fist.

I glance at my father one more time, and I'm about to say something when I realize…I have nothing to say to him. I turn back to Danny. "Let's go."

Chapter 12
Danny

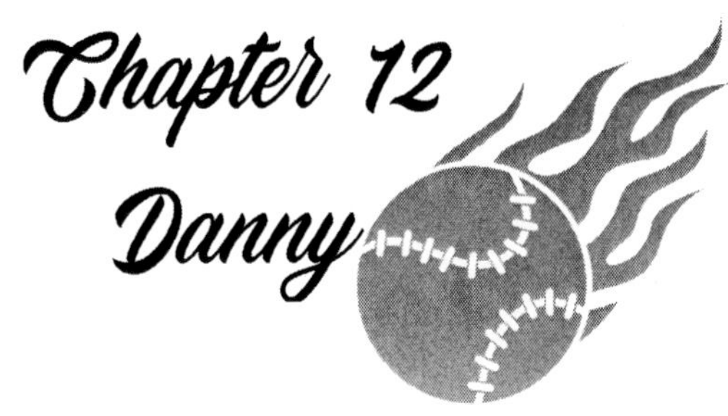

Paparazzi are sitting across the street, and they follow us as Alexis navigates the Yukon toward the nearest urgent care.

They follow us.

Shit.

This isn't what I need right now. I need to figure out what's wrong with my wrist and what the prognosis is, and I need to get in touch with Troy and the team medical staff before any of this hits the media.

And so I use my right hand to dial Troy as we head in that direction.

"Brewer, how was your Christmas?" he answers.

"Coach, I think I just broke my wrist."

His reply is silence at first followed by a low, "What?"

"I'm on my way to urgent care with Alexis Bodega and the paparazzi are following us. I wanted to inform you before it hits the media that we went to an urgent care together."

"Alexis Bod—" he begins, and he cuts himself off as he realizes that's not really the issue at hand right now. "How bad is it?"

"I can't make a fist without excruciating pain."

"Fuck. Any tingling up your arm?" he asks.

"No, I don't think so."

"What happened?"

"It's a long story, but basically my wrist broke my fall when another man fell on top of me, so the impact on my wrist was two grown men."

"What the fuck? How did another man fall on top of—oh Jesus, never mind," he mutters.

"It was Alexis's father. I married her last week, and he was trying to get the ring off my finger. He tripped into me and we both fell. It was an accident," I say, and I glance over at Alexis, who I realize hasn't heard the full story—until now, anyway.

She's silently driving while tears stream down her cheeks.

"I need to go, but can you notify the medical staff?" I ask him.

"Of course. Let me know the second you know how bad it is."

"Yes, Coach." I cut the call and set my phone in my lap.

"It was his fault?" she whispers through her tears.

"It was an accident."

She shakes her head. "He was trying to get the ring off your finger. You just said that."

"Yeah," I mutter. I'm trying to ride the line of protecting her and not lashing out at him, but it's a real thin fucking line. I'm not sure how much longer I can teeter on it.

"What else did he say?" she asks.

"It's all kind of a blur. Something about how they had it all set, and all you had to do was walk down the aisle, and then I ruined it all. He said I didn't deserve the ring, and that's when he kind of lunged for me. His intention wasn't to hurt me, it was to get the ring off my finger." I lift a shoulder, not sure how true those words are. Maybe his intention *was* to hurt me.

He didn't seem very sorry when he did.

We arrive at the parking lot of the urgent care, and she pulls into the space closest to the door. The paparazzi who followed us here—a grand total of three cars—screeches into the parking lot as we both rush out of the car, trying to beat them inside.

I'm sure someone snaps our photo. I'm sure there will be speculation all over the place.

I'm sure there already is after the Christmas special. We've stayed off social media, and we hunkered down for Christmas. I have no idea what's being said about us right now.

But the real world is waiting on the other side of this diagnosis.

The urgent care happens to only have two people waiting when we walk in, and Alexis marches right up to the desk. "We have a possible broken wrist that we'd like to get checked out," she says firmly but nicely.

The lady behind the desk stares at Alexis for a beat, clearly recognizing her, but then she hands over a clipboard like she would with any other patient. "Fill this out and bring it back up."

Alexis nods and takes the paperwork, and we sit down. She fills out the forms as she fires questions at me quietly in a corner, and she brings it back up a few minutes later. The other two patients have been called back, and my wrist throbs with pain as we wait.

The woman behind the desk asks for my insurance card, and I stand and turn so Alexis can get my wallet out of my pocket for me.

Her hands on my ass this way is not how I pictured this day going, that's for damn sure.

Eventually I'm called back, and I nod for Alexis to come with me. The medical assistant checks my vitals, asks several questions about how it happened, and then she lets us know the doctor will be right in.

He comes in a few minutes later. "Daniel Brewer, hello. I'm Dr. Hanson. Let's take a look at what you've got going on." He examines my wrist as pain rockets through me, and then he says, "My hunch is that it's broken, but let's get some x-rays."

We wait to get set up for the x-ray, and then we wait some more for the results.

I'm used to getting seen immediately by the team doctor. I haven't had to wait in an urgent care office since I was a kid.

I'm nervous as I wait. Nervous about what he's going to say. Nervous for how long this is going to keep me from playing the game I love. Nervous as to what all this means.

Eventually he returns. "The good news, Mr. Brewer, is that it's a clean distal radial fracture. You'll want to get an MRI with your team doctor to ensure there's no nerve or ligament damage, but from what I can tell, you're looking pretty lucky. I'm going to give you a temporary splint and let your doctor determine the next step for you."

"How long is this going to sideline me?" I ask quietly while he gets moving on the splint. He knows who I am. He knows that I play ball since we filled out that paperwork and he mentioned my team doctor.

"It depends on many factors, but my best estimate is six to eight weeks in a cast, another week or two in a splint, and then likely another couple weeks to build strength back."

"So we're looking at eight to twelve weeks?" I ask.

He nods. "I'm sorry, Mr. Brewer. I know that isn't the news you wanted to hear, and frankly, it's not what I wanted to tell you. I'm a fan."

"Thanks," I mutter. It's a nice sentiment, but it's not very helpful right now.

He finishes securing the splint in place around me as I hiss in pain. "Any other questions?" he asks.

I shake my head.

"I'll write you a prescription for hydrocodone to help ease the pain. If we can do anything else for you…" He hands me a business card.

I thank him, and then he heads out to write the prescription as my eyes lock on Alexis's.

"I'm so, so sorry, Danny," she whimpers.

"Hey, hey," I soothe, standing and taking her into my arms. "It's not your fault."

She folds herself into my chest, whimpering and clearly feeling bad about what her father did to me.

Meanwhile, I'm trying to figure out how I can use this to my advantage to get the information I want out of him.

And *that* is how I know that I'm truly a changed man.

This isn't going to come between us. This is just one more thing that's going to push us even harder into each other.

Chapter 13

Alexis

Guilt burrows inside of me.

This wouldn't have happened if he wasn't trying to protect me. He can call it an accident all he wants, but it wouldn't have happened if we didn't go to my father's house together today. It was an avoidable accident, but I guess that's what accidents are by nature.

And now after the initial diagnosis, he's not even going to get to participate in spring training. He might miss the first few games of the season.

It's my fault.

"What can I do?" I ask as we wait for the medical assistant to bring us his pain meds. I'm still buried in his chest, but I'm totally at a loss right now. I have no idea what to do to make any of this better.

He shakes his head. "You're doing it," he says.

I hold on a little tighter. "Are you doing okay?"

"I'm okay. It hurts like a motherfucker, but I'll live."

"We need to get you back to Vegas so you can meet with the team doctors," I say.

"Eventually. It's the day after Christmas. Nothing changes if I let them have a little time off."

"But you'll have answers. A timeline," I point out.

"The only timeline is living through it and letting it heal." His voice is low, and I can't tell how he feels about that.

I pray this doesn't drive a wedge between us, but I'm already scared it will. How can he *not* blame me when it's all I can think about?

The medical assistant comes back in with a pill bottle for Danny, and as she's explaining how to take the medication, my phone dings with a text.

I pull it out of my purse and see it's from Brooks.

Brooks: The paparazzi are swarming the urgent care and you two are all over the media. Hold tight while we figure out what to do.

My chest tightens.

This is it. We're all over the media. It's out there. There's no turning back now.

I share his text with Danny once the assistant leaves the room after telling us we're free to leave.

"What do you want to do?" he asks.

"Not listen to Brooks, that's for sure."

He chuckles. "Then let's go. We're pros at this by now, right?"

I nod, and we head out to the Yukon. I run to the driver's side while he heads to the passenger door, and we both hear our names being called. They want to know why we're here. They want to know what happened to Danny. They want to know what's going on between us.

They want every single intimate detail of our lives, but it's not theirs to have.

We ignore them as we get into the SUV, and I back carefully out of the spot—slowly so I don't hit anyone, though they're not exactly moving out of my way, and this is a freaking boat of a vehicle. Danny quietly navigates helpfully from the passenger seat, and I can tell he's itching to just do it himself.

But he's patient with me, and we make it onto the main road.

A line of cars follows us back to my dad's house, and when we arrive, I pull onto the driveway right in front of the front door.

It's not where we want to be right now, but it does offer a layer of protection.

I type the code into the keypad and let myself and Danny in through the front door. I'm not sure what we do next. Confront my father? Lay low for a few days?

Laying low here doesn't seem optimal for us personally, but it's probably our best course of action right now.

I just don't want my father around Danny. I won't want him poisoning the beauty we've created together. And I don't want to be here.

"I told you to hold tight," Brooks says. He's exasperated as he walks into the foyer.

"And I don't take orders from you, but thanks for the warning," I say dryly. "We made it here just fine."

He narrows his eyes at me, and he turns to walk away. He raises his voice down the hallway as he heads toward my father's study. "Raymond, your daughter has returned."

I roll my eyes, and then I follow in the direction he goes until I'm standing in the study.

"We need to make a statement," Brooks says. "I'm fielding calls left and right about what's going on."

"Then...don't pick up," I say, my tone indicating how obvious that answer is.

"It's my job to pick up," Brooks says thickly, and for the very first time in history, I almost think I see a backbone in the guy. "They want answers, and frankly, they deserve some. We all do."

"They deserve the truth." I flatten my lips as my answer is off the cuff, but as I think it through, I stand by it.

The Bodegiac community is a passionate, rabid fanbase who follows my career but also my personal life with dedication. They will stand behind me one hundred percent.

That community didn't come out of what my father built. It would be there regardless of whether Brooks was in my life.

They're here for *me*, and I've let my father brainwash me for far too long into believing they're only here for the brand.

I *am* my brand, and if they deserve some answers, then they deserve the truth.

"What part of the truth?" my father asks through gritted teeth.

"How about…all of it?" I say.

Danny stands by, silently observing our conversation.

I turn toward my father. "Aren't you going to ask him about the injury you caused?"

He looks shocked by my accusation. "The injury *I caused*? Are you kidding me right now?"

"You attacked him, and he broke his wrist because of it. Who knows what this means for *his* career, for *his* livelihood. It's bad enough you're trying to ruin mine."

"Oh, is that the tale he spun?" My dad shakes his head bitterly as his eyes flick to Danny. "I told you I'd ruin you. This is only the beginning."

"Stop it," I yell.

"Let's put this on the back burner for now," Brooks suggests, looking between my father and Danny, who's still silent. "We need to issue a statement *now* before things get out of hand."

"Then issue one," I say to him.

"It needs to come from you," he says.

"I'm sorry, but I don't have the time right now. My husband has a broken wrist, so I need to care for him. Come on, Danny," I say.

"Where are you going?" my dad asks.

"Anywhere but here," I mutter.

"Stop," he says, his voice forceful. "I will not let this come between us."

I spin around and face him. "Are you kidding me? It's far too late to be issuing those kinds of statements."

"Then just…stay here. For the next few days. Until the media circus dies down. You're safe here."

"Danny stays with me," I demand.

"Fine," he hisses, glaring at Danny. Wow, he really hates him.

"And apart from any discussions about business, you both leave us alone," I say, looking between Brooks and my dad.

"Fine," Brooks says, but my dad doesn't agree to it.

I raise both brows as I look at him.

"Fine," he relents. He looks defeated as he blows out a sigh, and for just the briefest moment, I connect a dot that I hadn't connected before.

He lost his wife, and all he's done since is hold tightly to his daughter to ensure he wouldn't lose her too.

It's not possible. In a way, it's delusional, really. She died after a long battle with an illness, but somehow, that translated to him taking control of my life—which was fine when I was a kid, and even when I was a teenager.

But he's refused for my entire life to let me flourish and grow on my own. He knows everything. He has all the answers.

He doesn't want me to learn any of them for myself.

And the harsh reality is that there's only one way I'll ever be able to escape it. I have to take control of my life. It may irreparably damage my relationship with my dad, but at least I'll have *my* life back—the way I *want* to live it instead of the way I'm *told* to live it.

And I want to share it with Danny. The rest? Just details.

"On one condition," my father adds.

"What?" I practically spit.

"You issue a statement now. One that Brooks and I draft," he says, nodding at my would-be husband.

I shake my head. "No deal. If I issue a statement, it will be one that *I* draft."

My father gives me a stern look, but we're far beyond stern looks at this point.

I clear my throat and speak the words that are in my heart. "I don't know what the future holds, but I do know that I can't continue working with two men who only care about what benefits them most."

"We have a contract," my father says thickly.

"A contract that is twelve years old," I protest. "I was *sixteen* when I signed that."

"I spoke to a lawyer a few days ago," Danny says.

I turn toward him with my jaw slackened. "You did?"

"My job as your husband is to protect you, so I reached out to a friend with some questions." He shrugs, and he's so…perfect. He's my knight in freaking shining armor riding in on his horse to save the day when I'm least expecting it.

"What did he say?" I ask.

"I learned that coercing a teenager into signing a contract is not only unfair but also unconscionable. The terms of perpetuity that appear to be a significant part of the contract create a power imbalance, and you'll be hard-pressed to find a court that would uphold your terms, particularly in the case of someone who's as successful as your daughter is."

"There was no coercion," my dad says. "She signed it freely and willingly, and she was fine with it until she met you. What would the courts have to say about that?"

Danny faces off with my father. "What does your daughter have to say about that?" He shrugs, and he's so casual, so collected, as he confronts the man who broke his wrist earlier today. God, I love him. "I'll be honest, Mr. Bodega. She wasn't fine with it until she met me. She just finally met someone who supported her and loved her enough to allow her to use her own voice. And the things she uses that voice for are pretty fucking incredible. You'd be so proud of her if you ever shut up long enough to listen."

My dad flinches as if he's been physically struck, and I have never loved Danny more than this moment right here.

Whatever happens with my dad over the next couple of days doesn't matter.

I've got Danny in my corner, and that may be all I need.

Chapter 14
Danny

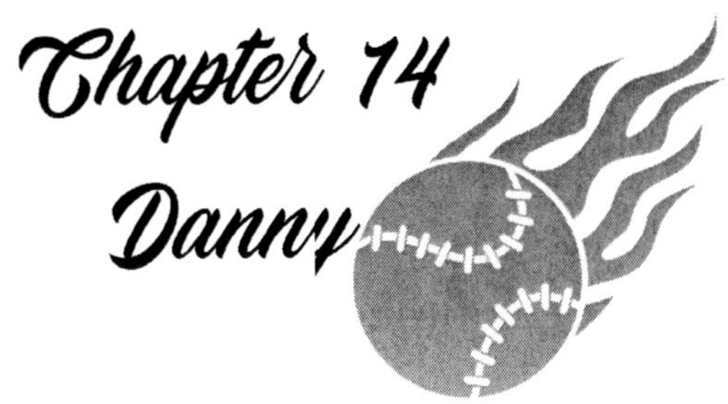

"No statement," Alexis says firmly, facing off against these two men. "This is my life we're talking about, and I don't have a statement to make right now. It's personal."

"You ran out on your wedding, and now you're traipsing all around town with the baseball player," her father argues.

The way he says *baseball player* as if it's some virus grates on my nerves. I'm already angry with the guy for what he's done to me, and now he's hurling insults.

"People deserve to know what's going on," he says.

"Oh, you mean I should let everyone know how you blackmailed me into marrying Brooks despite my protests? You want people to know that?" she asks.

He glares at her as he presses his lips together, and I try to get another look at the paper sitting on her father's desk, but I can't tell if it's the same paper from before or not. Surely if it was something he didn't want us to see, it wouldn't be sitting out on his desk still.

In the chaos of breaking my wrist, it left my mind. But it's back now, burning a hole in my brain.

People don't keep paper trails these days, but he's from a different generation than me. Maybe he does.

I crane my neck a little to get a glimpse of it without being obvious. It has a lot of words and some numbers on it, but I'm too far away to get a good look. Maybe I can sneak back in here later to get a better look.

"What about a quick video checking in, maybe wishing happy holidays?" I suggest. "Then they can see for themselves you're okay without you having to make a statement about your personal life."

She glances thoughtfully at me. "I love that idea. Let's do it."

"Fine. Let's sit by the Christmas tree in the foyer," her father suggests.

Is this my chance? I stay in the back of the crowd as they all head toward the foyer, and I take a step back toward the desk to try to get a look.

Alexis stops and turns around to look at me. "You okay?"

I nod, and now that I've been caught, I follow the group out of the study and to the foyer to record this video.

I never get the chance to get back in there, and I can't help but think this has been the day from hell as I lay in bed beside my wife.

And now I'm sleeping in my enemy's house…or rather, not sleeping, as the case may be.

I just never thought my enemy would turn out to be my father-in-law. Or my father. What the fuck is the deal with fathers?

I realize now as I lie awake, my wrist throbbing in pain despite the Lortab I took before bed, that the only father figure either of us can depend on right now is Gregory.

I thought the pain meds were supposed to make me sleepy.

Instead, I feel wired.

I check the clock. It's after two in the morning.

I get up, and Alexis doesn't move. She's sleeping, and I think to myself...*maybe this is my chance.*

I slip out of the bedroom and head down to the study.

The door is open, and frankly, I'm surprised the door isn't locked. I use the flashlight on my phone as I sneak into the office and behind the desk, moving quickly to try to find that paper from earlier. The top of the desk has many papers on it, so I can't tell if there's something useful here to figure out what's going on with her father or not. Mostly it's contacts for Bodega Talent Agency, and that's when I see another paper with *Bodega Investment Portfolio* across the top.

Just as I pick it up, I hear footsteps down the hall.

My heart races as I slip down onto the floor and hide under the huge executive desk.

The light flicks on.

Oh, shit.

Did someone see me come in here?

I stay as silent as possible.

"I said two-fifteen on the dot, Raymond." I hear Brooks's voice first.

"Yeah, yeah. What do you want me to do now?" Raymond asks. The door latches shut. They're talking in here in what they think is privacy. They have no idea I'm just a few feet away under the desk, listening to every word.

I silently open my phone and start a video, praying I'll pick up their voices.

"The terms still stand. Get the merger to go through, and I'll pay back your losses. Get your daughter to marry me, and I'll double them."

I stifle a grunt of surprise. Brooks is the bad guy? All this time I just thought he was a dorky loser. I had no idea he was the one orchestrating all of this. Somehow he slid under the radar while we put the full blame on her father.

He's not innocent by any means, but seeing him shoulder the blame with Brooks is a little shocking, to say the least.

"The losses are your fault, Brooks," he hisses.

"It was your bad investments, Mr. Bodega, not mine."

"I was doing you a favor! And this is how you repay me?"

"We've worked well together for many years. Don't let this ruin our relationship now. You know I'm better for your daughter than that scummy baseball trash," Brooks says.

Scummy baseball trash?

I hurl a silent insult at that asshole. *Fuck you!*

"You know the future is in a huge conglomerate of D-Three and Bodega Talent." Brooks continues. "DB-Three Industries has a nice ring to it, don't you think? And a cushy COO position for you. A nice paycheck. You can still run your daughter's career. Or ruin it, as the case may be."

"The merger can still happen without the marriage," Raymond says. "I'll admit I got greedy when I thought I could get her to marry you, but she's better off where she is now. At least Brewer is trying to protect her, which is more than I can say for you."

My chest tightens.

Does her dad…actually not hate me?

"Don't be like that, Raymond," Brooks chides. "We've worked hard to get Alexis into the position she's in today, and she'll easily make back her money with her next album. You know we both have a lot to gain from her success."

"If she lets us continue working for her," Raymond points out. "She's onto us, and that baseball player is, too. It won't be long before they put it together, and where does that leave us?"

"You were stupid to let her out of your sight long enough to get tangled up with him," Brooks says.

"I didn't," her father protests. "Gregory did."

"Which is why he's no longer employed."

"Actually, he is. She hired him. Regardless, they're sniffing around," Raymond says. "They'll know soon enough that I didn't freeze anything but that it's all gone. And then what?"

"That sounds like a *you* problem, Ray. Have a good night."

I hear the door open, and Brooks leaves. I wait with bated breath to see whether her father is going to come around to this side of the desk. I hear his hand as he slaps it down hard onto his desk, and then he lets out a long, frustrated sigh before the light flicks off and he walks out of the study, too.

I stop the recording on the phone.

So that's the truth.

Brooks is blackmailing Raymond because he lost all of Alexis's money with bad investments he made to somehow help Brooks.

This leaves me with a lot of questions, though. Why does Brooks want to marry Alexis so badly? And how else did Raymond lose her money? What bad investments did he make and how did it help Brooks?

I don't have those answers…yet.

But now that I know at least a part of the truth…what the fuck am I supposed to do with it?

Chapter 15
Danny

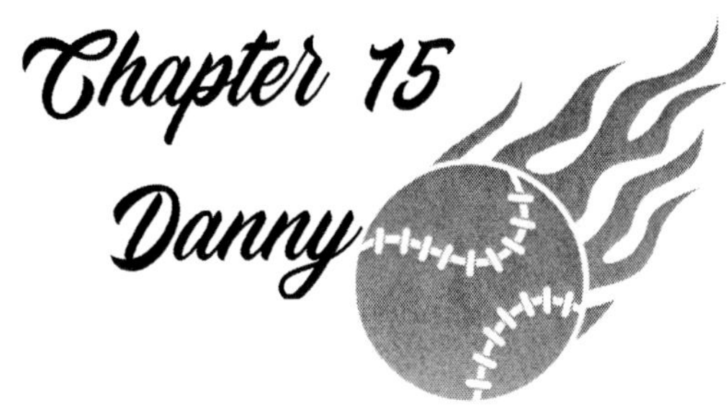

I return to bed, and Alexis has no idea I was ever gone. Now I don't sleep for a completely different reason…well, on top of the throbbing, constant ache in my wrist.

I wrestle with what to do. There's definitely more to the story. There's no way he blew all of Alexis's money on investments with Brooks. I'm fairly certain she was nearing billionaire status, so if he did, I can't even fathom that horrific mismanagement of someone else's money, though it's happened before with agents. I recall hearing about a documentary featuring boy bands where their agent basically swindled them out of the money they deserved.

That's not what happened here, exactly…but it does ring a little too similar for my own liking.

I want to tell her. I need to tell her. But I also need to protect her, and right now, those are two conflicting ideals.

I can't tell her and protect her. I can't tell her all her money is gone until I know whether her dad has a way to get the merger to go through to get his money back.

And I need to know more about the financial status of Bodega Talent, too. Did he blow all his money for the company? Or just Alexis's money?

It's only six when I finally get out of bed. I head downstairs and consider taking a run around the neighborhood to burn off some nervous energy, but when I look out the front window, the paparazzi are still parked across the street.

Jesus.

I feel like a prisoner in here. I can't imagine how she's felt all these years.

I wander to the kitchen, and I spot a Keurig, so I poke around until I find a pod and set myself up.

"Help yourself," a voice behind me says dryly.

I spin around to find Raymond. I'm about to offer some snappy retort about how he can afford it, but then I realize…maybe he can't.

I snap my jaw shut, but then I open it again and words tumble out of me before I get a chance to stop them. "I know what you're doing, and you're not going to get away with it."

"I don't know what the hell you're talking about," he mutters. He moves past me to the refrigerator and takes out some orange juice.

"Your investments with Brooks," I clarify. "Spending all Alexis's money. Forcing the merger so Brooks will pay you back. None of that's ringing a bell?"

He freezes but only for a second, careful to cover his tracks. "Nope."

"Interesting. What I can't figure out is *why*, though. I mean, I get why he'd want to merge companies—so he can rule the world, obviously. But what about marrying her? Why would he want that? All I could come up with as I tossed and turned, not easy with only one working arm, mind you, was that he'd get a cut of future profits that way—particularly if *you* drafted the prenup since she always trusted you. Which, obviously, was her first mistake." I say it all so casually, mostly as a way to piss him off.

"You have no idea what you're talking about."

I slide my phone out of my pocket and hit play on the video from last night. The voices are far away, but if I blast my volume, it's audible.

Brooks's voice is clear as the conversation begins. "I said two-fifteen on the dot, Raymond."

We hear what Raymond said next, and then I turn off the video and slide my phone back into my pocket.

"You still want to deny it?" I ask.

He sighs. "Where'd you get that?"

"It doesn't matter."

"Apple doesn't fall far from the tree, huh?" he asks.

"What do you mean?" My brows draw together at his insinuation.

"Your old man recorded you and Alexis without your knowledge or consent. You recorded me. Same thing."

"I'm nothing like my father," I hiss.

"Could've fooled me." Now *he* is the casual one, and it's doing nothing but pissing me the fuck off. "You think I didn't know he had a sex tape with the two of you? You think I didn't know you've been sneaking around with my daughter for months?"

"Why didn't you try to stop it if you knew?" I ask.

"I did try to stop it," he snaps. "And that's how I learned Gregory is a fucking traitor."

"Gregory is the most loyal man I've ever met in my life. He was hired to protect Alexis *by* Alexis, and that's all I've ever seen him do. But I get how that would seem traitorous to you since he didn't have *your* best interests in mind." I shrug.

"Oh, come off it. We all know he's boinking your mom."

I'm about to slug him for his vulgarity when we both hear humming coming down the hallway. There's only one person I know who hums from the moment she wakes up in the morning, and it's the angel who appears in the doorway a beat later.

"Good morning," she says, and she walks over toward me, essentially ignoring her father. "How's your wrist today?"

"I'll live," I say dryly. "How'd you sleep?"

"Good. You?"

"Fine," I lie. My coffee is done, and I grab it and drink it black. It's bitter, but it gives me a little energy to get moving on my day.

"Good morning, sweetheart," her dad says as if he hasn't completely ruined our lives.

"Morning," she says, essentially ignoring him as she sets about making breakfast. He walks out of the room, and I feel very much like our conversation was left unfinished.

He knows I know.

I'm not sure what he plans to do about it, though.

She sets a plate in front of me with an egg white omelet and some whole wheat toast a few minutes later. It's not bacon, but it'll do.

I scarf it down. "I'm going to attempt to shower. Not sure how that's going to work out with this thing on." I hold up my wrist.

"Do you need some help?"

"I wouldn't say no to my wife joining me in the shower…"

She laughs. "Give me a couple of minutes. I'm going to call Gregory and check in with him."

I nod. "I may stop by your dad's study for a word with him, too."

She gives me a curious look but seems to let it go as she nods. "Good luck."

I head toward the study, and I find him perched behind his desk. He looks up at me over his glasses when I stand in the doorway.

"Can I ask you a favor?" he asks.

I clear my throat. "Depends."

"Don't say anything to her yet. Whatever you think you know…you don't. Okay? It's complicated. Give me a chance to figure out my next move."

"I won't keep secrets from my wife for anybody, least of all you," I retort.

"Then I will ruin you," he snarls.

"Bring it on," I say cheerfully, and I walk out of his stupid office and up the stairs to take my shower.

Before I get in, though, my phone starts to ring. When I see it's my mother calling, I pick up the call.

"Hey, Mom."

"Hey, honey," she says quietly. "Listen, I know Gregory and Alexis are talking now, so I just wanted to give you a quick call."

"You doing okay?" I ask.

"Well, yes, but I called for another reason."

"What is it?" My chest tightens with alarm.

She sighs. "It's your father. I just got word that he's in the hospital and he's fighting for his life. He's not doing well, Danny. If you have something you want to say to him, now might be the right time to say it."

"Oh," I say, not really sure how to respond. I'm not sure I actually *do* have anything I want to say to him. I think I've said it all at this point. "Okay. Thanks."

"He's at Alhambra. You okay?"

"Uh, yeah. I'm okay. I already knew he was sick, so it's not a shock or anything."

"Why were you at urgent care yesterday?" she asks, shifting topics abruptly. "It's all over the news that Alexis Bodega escorted Danny Brewer into an urgent care in California. Couldn't you, you know, pay for a doctor to come to you?"

"I broke my wrist," I say flatly. "Any doctor that came to me wouldn't have had an x-ray machine on short notice."

"Oh, Danny," she murmurs, her tone apologetic. "How bad is it?"

"It's a clean break, but even so, I'll be out eight to twelve weeks. I'll miss spring training and opening day. I need to follow up with the team medical staff to double check for nerve or ligament damage."

"Oh no. I'm so sorry. How did it happen?" she asks.

I debate whether to get into it right now. I debate a lot of things in a split second, actually.

Like whether I should call Gregory with what I know.

He knows how to neutralize people. Maybe he can neutralize Raymond.

"It was accidental," I finally say. I'm not protecting Raymond, but it's true.

It wouldn't have happened if he wasn't trying to attack me, but the actual break itself was my own fault for sticking my hand out to break our fall. I guess breaking my wrist is better than fucking up my entire back, which would've been the alternative.

"Well you know I'm here if you need anything at all," she says.

"I know." We end the call, and I send Gregory a text.

Me: I learned some interesting information last night. Listen when you're alone. I haven't told her anything yet. Let's find time to talk.

I attach the video and hope for the best.

Chapter 16
Alexis

My call with Gregory is quick, but I figure Danny will be in the shower by the time I make it upstairs.

He's still sitting on the bed when I walk in. His phone is off and on the bed in front of him, but he's staring at it like it's on fire.

"What's going on?" I ask, sitting beside him.

"My mom called before I got in the shower. My, uh…my *dad* is in the hospital and I guess it's not looking good. She said if I have anything to say to him, I should go say it."

"Oh, Danny. I'm so sorry." I reach over and take his good hand in mine. "Are you okay?"

"Everyone keeps asking me that, and…yeah. I'm fine. He's been as good as dead to me for the last twenty years anyway. Or worse than that, even, since all he's managed to do in the last twenty years is either ask for money or make my life hell."

I pull the back of his hand to my lips for a quick kiss. "As someone who has lost a parent, I can attest to the fact that there is absolutely no wrong way to deal with this type of thing. Some moments you'll feel fine. Other moments you won't." I shrug. "It's all normal."

He presses his lips together and nods. "Thanks."

"Do you have anything to say to him?"

"I'm not sure," he admits.

"Do you think you'll regret it if you don't make peace with him while you still can?"

His eyes flick from his phone up to mine. "I don't know."

"If you're not sure, then there's a chance you *will* end up with regrets. And I don't want that for you."

He closes his eyes for a beat and nods. "Then let's go."

"You want me to come with you?"

He nods. "I can't go alone."

"Of course."

"Help me shower first?" he asks.

I carefully wrap his arm in a garbage bag and wrap a towel around that, and then I help him in the shower.

A half hour later, we pull out of the driveway to head toward the hospital.

We're followed out of the neighborhood by three cars again, and I should've really thought ahead to the fact that we went to an urgent care yesterday and a hospital today.

I wouldn't think the paparazzi would be so brazen as to follow us into the hospital to figure out why we're going there, but you really never know.

Danny is silently lost in thought for the entire forty minute drive there, and I let him think through what he wants to say to his dad. If he needs to say something or get an opinion from me, he'll ask.

I slide into a parking spot, and I glance over at him. "You ready?"

He presses his lips together and nods. "As ready as I'll ever be."

The three cars that followed us here snap photos of us as we walk from the parking lot into the building, and I wish I had it in me to care about what they're going to say about us for the highest price.

I hate that someone is making money off my private life as I walk into a hospital to say goodbye to the man who is by law my father-in-law, but it's part of what I chose when I chose this life.

Danny got the room number from his mom, and we stop at the desk to get directions. The guard working there stares at me with his jaw dropped, but he's working at a hospital. He knows better than to point out that Alexis Bodega just walked into the room as Danny tells him he's looking for Peter Brewer's room.

We find the room, and it's empty of visitors when we walk in. The man I've met one other time is lying on the bed staring up at the ceiling, a tube under his nose helping him breathe. He looks weaker than the first time I saw him, which really wasn't all that long ago.

"What are you doing here?" he asks. There's no life to his tone. It's not a demand. It's not curious. It's just flat.

"Where are your wife and kids?" Danny asks.

"The wife went to get lunch with the kids. They're here," he says, a touch of defensiveness to his tone. "Now what is it you came here for?"

"Came to tell you that for as much as you've made my life hell, I forgive you," Danny says. His tone is a little lifeless, too—as if he's saying some words he rehearsed but possibly doesn't mean them.

And I don't blame him for not meaning them. His dad doesn't deserve forgiveness for the things he's done to his son.

"Okay," his father says.

I don't know what I was expecting, but I don't think it was that.

"Do you have anything to say to me?" Danny asks.

He lifts a shoulder. "I accept your forgiveness."

Danny's fingers flex on his good hand, and I reach over and take his hand in mine, standing firm in solidarity with him. This is a moment for his father to tell him he's sorry for the way he's treated Danny, but clearly he's not.

"I also wanted to let you know that all your files have been wiped. You no longer have that tape. You have no hold over me."

"Oh, you think I don't have other copies saved?" he sneers, the most energy we've seen come from him in the short time he's been here.

"When was the last time you checked?" Danny asks.

His father doesn't have an answer to that, and clearly it was before he got here to the hospital—whenever that was.

"Yeah," Danny says. "That's what I thought. At least that video dies with you now." He doesn't say it, exactly, but we all know it'll be soon.

"I guess so. So you outsmarted me. Congratulations," he says. His voice is weak again, and he coughs at the end, the brutal type of cough that makes me scared he's going to cough up blood or vomit, but he draws in a deep breath from the tube and it seems to do the trick.

"I thought you'd want to make amends considering where you are. I guess I was wrong, and that's a real shame, Pete. I gave you a chance. I said what I needed to say. And now…I guess we'll go. Good luck. Hope I don't see you on the other side." Danny spins to leave, and Peter's voice stops him cold.

"I'm sorry."

Danny stares straight ahead at the door without responding.

"I should have handled things differently. I should have lived differently. I know that now, and I hope you know how hard that is for me to admit."

Danny turns around slowly, his eyes meeting mine on the way. He looks shocked. "I know. And thank you for saying it."

His father nods, and Danny walks over and sets his hand on his dad's arm. "I wish things could have been different, but I want to leave in peace."

"What happened to your arm?" his dad asks, as if he just noticed Danny's brace.

"I broke my wrist." He clears his throat.

"Shit. How long is the recovery?"

"I'll probably miss a few games." Danny shrugs.

"I watched all your games," Peter murmurs. "I was a shitty father, but I watched every game I could."

"Thanks," Danny mutters. Neither of them is used to these tender moments. "I got into ball because of you. You know that, right?"

His father grunts.

"You showed me how to throw a ball, but it was Mom who kept me playing." He clears his throat again.

"Keep winning," his dad says.

"I'll do my best."

"And Alexis?" his dad adds.

I snap to attention. "Yes?"

"I'm sorry for what I did to you, too. You got dragged into an old fight, and you deserved better."

"Thank you." I'm not quite sure what else to say. Get well soon seems inappropriate given what we know. "I'm glad we were able to visit today."

"We'll go before everyone gets back, but we'll be thinking of you," Danny says.

"Thanks." Peter closes his eyes again as we leave the room, and for some reason, I feel a sense of relief as we walk out of the room.

Danny took care of the video, and his dad is no longer in a position to share it anyway.

There's a lot of peace in that itself, but the fact that they had that conversation—whether or not Danny really forgives him—

is a step toward giving Danny the peace he deserves where his father is concerned.

"I'm proud of you," I say softly as we head back toward the Yukon.

The paparazzi are still out there snapping photos, and we rush over to the vehicle to try to avoid as many photos as we can. I navigate toward home, and when we get there, my dad is waiting for us.

"Really? Going to the hospital together the day after urgent care? Did you think this wasn't going to immediately hit the media?" he demands.

I toss my hands in the air. "I'm so tired of not living my life because of whatever image we're portraying or whatever explanation you think we owe the world. We don't owe anybody anything."

Danny sighs.

"Well, we have to make a statement now," my dad says.

"No, we don't. And I won't."

"Then I will," he hisses.

"Do what you have to do," I spit back at him, and I storm upstairs to my bedroom.

I'm ready to get the hell out of this house. Pronto.

But I never realized the can of worms I'd be opening with my words to my father.

Chapter 17
Alexis

"On behalf of my client and daughter, Alexis Bodega, I'm happy to announce that she's safe and healthy. Her husband, baseball player Daniel Brewer, suffered a broken wrist. She's been by his side caring for him, so I'm here today to dispel rumors that something is wrong with her. Thank you for your time."

I sit up in my bed and watch it again just to be sure I heard all that correctly.

Is he fucking kidding me?

Danny sits up beside me to watch it, too.

He not only announced my marriage to the world in that little statement of his, but he also announced to the world that Danny has a broken wrist—before he's even had a chance to tell his teammates, his agent, his management team…

What a disaster.

When I told my father to do what he had to do, I certainly didn't mean this. I thought he'd let people know I'm fine. Helping a friend, or something along those lines.

This is only going to make things worse. Since we haven't announced anything yet, we'll be fielding calls about our marriage, when it happened, when we met, how it happened—on top of how Danny broke his wrist, how long he'll be out, if he's thinking about early retirement, blah blah blah.

And to make matters worse, everyone knows I was supposed to marry Brooks a couple weeks ago, and now I turn up married to Danny.

If my father was concerned about my image and brand, he's absolutely going the wrong way about trying to make anything better.

And he knows it. He said he'd ruin Danny, and he's so blinded by his desire to do it that he isn't considering the huge ramifications his words will have on me. He knows my only choice is to make a statement of my own countering his, and that's why he did it.

To force my hand.

Well, he's not going to like what I have to say next, that's for *damn* sure.

"What do you want to do?" Danny asks. His voice sounds tired, and to be completely honest, I wouldn't blame him if he just wanted to throw in the towel at this point. My father has done nothing but make things difficult for us over the course of our relationship, and really, all this is still relatively new.

We're still getting to know each other.

We're still in the honeymoon phase.

But my dad is trying his hardest to rip all that out from under us.

"I'm sorry, Danny," I say quietly.

He purses his lips and shakes his head, and then he sinks back into his pillows. "It's not your fault. He said he was coming for me, and, well, here we are."

"It's been a crap day, hasn't it?"

"I sort of made amends with my dad, and it feels good to just let that shit go." He shrugs, and he sucks in a deep breath before he lets it go. "I need to tell you something."

He seems a little nervous, and it makes me nervous.

"What?" I ask.

He draws in a long breath. "I couldn't sleep last night, and I went downstairs at two in the morning. I went into your dad's study because he'd been acting suspicious with a piece of paper, so I was looking around his desk to try to figure out what it was. I didn't find it, but I heard voices coming into the study, so I jumped under his desk. He and Brooks were talking."

My face scrunches up as I come to terms with that. "At two in the morning?"

"They were having a secret meeting they clearly didn't want either of us to hear."

"What did they say?" I ask, my heart suddenly thundering in my chest.

He sucks his bottom lip into his mouth for a beat, and that's when I know this is bad.

Really bad.

"I was going to wait to tell you. I wanted to gather more information since right now I feel like I'm missing some key pieces."

"What do you know?" I demand, my voice about an octave higher than usual.

"Brooks is a douchebag and he's blackmailing your dad."

My brows pinch together. "For what?"

"I guess your dad made some bad investments, and Brooks said he'd pay those back for him if he got the merger to go through. And he'd pay double if your father could get you to marry him."

"Bad investments?" I repeat. "What bad investments?"

"That's the part I'm missing. He said something about how he did it as a favor to Brooks in the first place."

"So *Brooks* is the bad guy in all this?" I screech. "Brooks?"

He nods. "Looks like it."

"So why are my assets frozen?"

He clears his throat. "I don't think they are, Alexis. I think they're just…" He trails off as he lifts a shoulder.

"Gone?" I say almost as a joke.

But then he starts to nod slowly, and my heart sinks somewhere into the pit of my stomach.

"I'm so sorry. But…yeah. Anything your dad was managing looks like it's gone."

"Holy shit," I murmur, my heart racing. "He manages most of it. Including payments to Gregory."

"Then you need to talk to him and figure out where your money went."

"Does he know you know?" I ask.

He nods. "He told me not to say anything to you until he could figure out what to do, but I told him I wasn't going to keep secrets from you."

My racing heart seems to calm a little at that. If nothing else, I have Danny on my side.

But if all my money is gone…

How do I fund my next tour?

How do I fund my next album?

How do I buy that house in San Diego?

I might have some solutions…but I definitely don't have them all.

"Let's not tell him I know yet," I say. "I want to see what move he makes next."

He nods. "I'm on board for whatever you think is the right way to handle this. And I want to add one more thing." He pauses, and then he says, "Your dad really does care about you, Lex. I know it's hard to see it right now, but he's pissed about you running off and marrying me. Someday he'll see the light. I have faith in that."

"What makes you say that?"

"He said last night that I'm better for you than Brooks."

I gasp. "He said what?" Of all the confessions he just made, that one might be the most shocking.

He nods. "He said at least I'm trying to protect you. And, for the record, I am. And I always will."

I reach over and squeeze his hand. "I know you will. And that's why my heart found you and decided it would never let go."

He leans forward and slides his hand around my neck, pulling me down for a kiss.

I lose myself in his kiss for a bit.

There's an awful lot we're up against, but I just have this feeling that we'll fight through it together.

Chapter 18
Danny

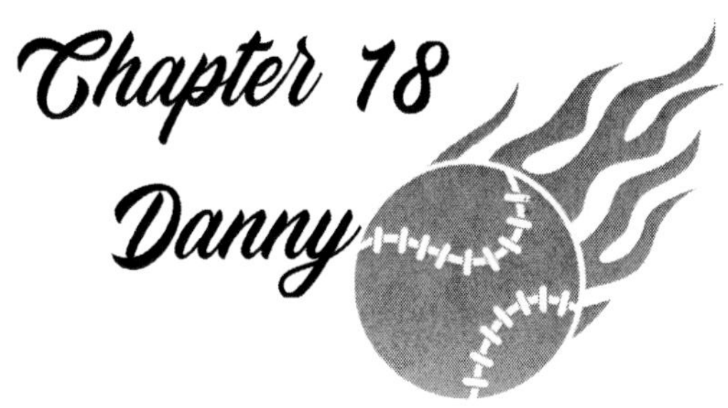

It was Alexis's idea for me to confront her dad to see if I could fill in the gaps, and honestly, I don't *want* to confront him. I'm pissed he announced my injury to the world. It was a dick move, and I already had to calm Brad down when he called me asking if it was true.

He wants me to hold a press conference.

I refuse.

First of all, I'm in Los Angeles. But on top of that, I don't want to sit there while the media fires questions about how long I'm going to be out when I don't have that estimate yet. Troy can field that one as soon as we have more answers, and that's what I tell Brad.

Beyond that, I'm not really up for discussing the implications that come with a serious injury. I don't want to get emotional about how I'm going to miss spring training for the first time in my career. I don't want to feel the weight of missing the first few games after we just won the World Series.

But I do want answers from the man who decided it was his right to share my personal life and struggles with the media, and I head down to his study the next morning with the attitude that he owes me after what he did to me.

"Can I have a few minutes of your time?" I ask when I walk into the sprawling study.

He raises a brow and doesn't really respond, but I take it as my green light, shutting the door behind me.

I walk in slowly and sit in the chair opposite him, the desk separating us. "We saw your statement. It wasn't your right to announce our marriage nor my injury." I keep the emotion out of my voice even though my fist keeps involuntarily clenching at my side.

"You told me to do what I had to do. That was what I had to do." His tone is detached, too.

"You didn't *have* to do it that way," I point out. "And because you did, I think the least you could do is answer a few questions I have."

He looks nearly impressed that I have the balls to come in here and fire questions at him, but he doesn't respond.

I take that as my cue to plow forward. "Look, you already know I know the basics, so I just need you to fill in a few blanks for me. I might even be able to help you if I know what's going on," I say.

He leans back in his chair and folds his arms over his chest. "What do you want to know?"

"I want to know what investments you're blaming on Brooks."

"Venture capitalism."

"Start-up companies?" I clarify.

He nods. "Brooks had friends with ideas. They were looking for seed funding from a limited partner to fund their startups. The good news is that I'm only out the money I invested, unlike general partners. But the bad news is that every single one of the startups he threw my way ultimately failed."

"So…you spent all of Alexis's money on startups with no guarantees?"

He shakes his head. "I reinvested a lot of money into Bodega Talent. It costs money to attract big-name clients."

"Alexis being a client doesn't sell your agency for you?"

"It doesn't really work like that," he says. "It doesn't hurt us, but the rumors were already swirling that Alexis was unhappy at Bodega. And if the CEO's own daughter is unhappy, that doesn't bode well for someone unrelated."

I'm surprised he's being so candid. "So it was bad business practices combined with bad investments?"

He purses his lips as he nods. "It was the perfect storm. But if the merger went through with D-Three, I would've been set. Brooks would've paid back my losses for the bad investments, and I would've made bank out of the dividends. Double if I got her to marry him."

"Right. But why did he want to marry her if he didn't love her?" I ask.

"Marriage isn't just about love, Daniel. It's also a partnership, and it's that partnership Brooks was after."

My brows dip. "Like…a companion?" Brooks was just lonely this whole time? Hell, I've got plenty of women on speed dial who could've taken care of that.

"No, not a companion. A *partnership*. He stood to gain a shitload of benefits if he married her."

"Financial?" I press.

"Well, yeah. Financial security is a big one. He's not hurting there, though. So as her husband, he was also set to benefit in terms of social status and business credibility. And talk about networking opportunities…" He shakes his head a little.

"Thank you for your candor. But can I ask you one final question?"

He shrugs. He didn't give me permission to ask the first few, yet he's here giving me answers.

"Why did *you* agree to it?"

He grunts out a chuckle, but it's almost maniacal in nature. "I saw the writing on the wall. I made bad investments. Ultimately that falls on me—whether or not he talked me into it, regardless of the reasons why I did it, I was the one signing off on those deals. It seemed like the only way to make her money back."

"So how much of it is gone? All of it?" I can't help as the question slips out.

"I believe you said the previous question was your last."

I nod, and I stand. Before I leave, though, I say, "Why'd you answer me?"

He glances down at his desk before his eyes return to mine. "Apart from feeling a little guilty about the wrist, I think you might be my only remaining direct line to my daughter."

I press my lips together and nod. So he fucked up, but at least he's man enough to admit it. I want to ask if he's stolen money from any of his other clients or just his daughter, but I leave it be.

For now.

Chapter 19
Alexis

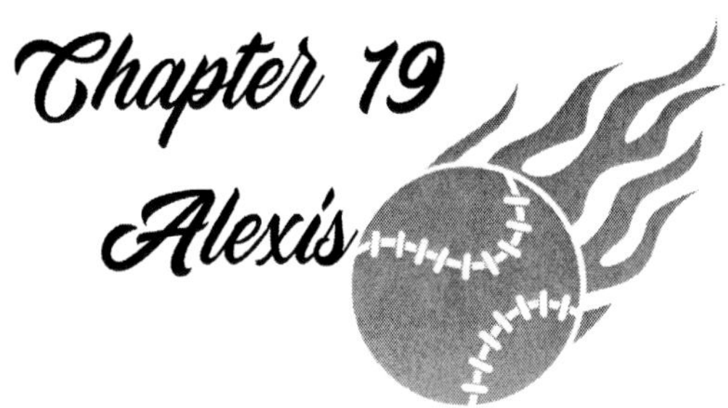

"Wow," I breathe as he finishes telling me everything he just found out as we sit together on my bed, leaning up against the headboard. "So, just to be clear, as far as my father's concerned…I'm broke?"

The words feel weighty coming out of my mouth. I can't really believe it's true, but I do have a few of my own accounts my father never knew about. I've been careful to keep my own separate money mostly because Gregory told me I could never be too safe.

And now I can't help but wonder how much he knew.

I have a lot of different investments, and I'll be okay. I can still buy that house I wanted—just not with the financing options Gregory used when he was trying to help me make the purchase.

I'm angry. I'm hurt. I'm anxious.

But I'm also feeling a big sense of determination.

Knowing what my father's done puts me squarely back in the driver's seat.

"As far as he's concerned?" he asks.

I nod. "He doesn't know about a few of my own accounts. I'll be okay, Danny. But he doesn't need to know that."

He presses his lips together and nods. "Of course you will. You're smart, talented, and independent despite what he tried to pull. And he didn't answer the question of how much of your money he spent, but he did admit he made some bad investments with the agency and also with these companies Brooks got him to invest in."

I let out a low whistle. It's even worse than I first thought.

But at the same time...we're still living in the same mansion, so we must not be flat broke yet.

Or Brooks is footing the bill.

Brooks. Just the mere thought of his name makes my stomach twist violently.

I thought he was on our side. I thought he was a decent guy.

Truth be told, I didn't think he had enough of a backbone to do what he did.

I'll give him credit for that, I guess. The rest is just kind of mind blowing, though. "We need to find a way to get back at Brooks for what he's done. We need to bleed him dry."

"Well, you could start by moving to a new management company," Danny suggests.

I nod. "I know of a few. Leila Monroe is always bragging about her management company. Maybe I could call her and fish around for some information. Maybe even suggest a merger with that company. If my dad merges with them first, he can't merge with D-Three."

"True, but I'm not sure that's exactly how it all works. But calling and fishing isn't a bad idea. You could see if she's heard anything about Bodega Talent, too."

I nod, and I grab my phone and dial her before I lose my nerve.

"Alexis Bodega! How the hell have you been?" she answers, and I laugh.

"It's complicated," I deadpan, our usual greeting for one another.

"Here too, girl. What's going on?"

"Quick question, and I'm asking for a friend. Is your manager taking new clients?"

"A friend, huh?" she asks, her tone full of disbelief.

"Yes, a friend."

"Why aren't you recommending Brooks's company?"

I sigh. "It's complicated."

She chuckles. "Danny Brewer complicated?"

"Okay, so it's not actually that complicated. Yes, the rumors are true. I married him a few days ago, and I've never been happier. And I want to leave D-Three and find new management," I admit.

"Well congratulations, my friend. Are you looking for a new agent, too?"

I've never spoken a word to Leila about my dad being my agent. She's nice enough, but you can't be too careful with personal things like that. "Why would you ask that?"

"Are you leaving your dad's company?" she presses rather than answering me.

"I…uh, I don't know."

"Honey, rumors that Bodega is going down are all over the place right now. If he can't hold onto his own daughter as a client, how's he going to hold onto anybody else? Everybody had eyes on the merger with D-Three. We're all waiting for it to happen, and we assumed it didn't because of the holidays…but I don't know. Something smells fishy. First you ran out on your wedding to your manager, then you show up married after rumors were swirling that nobody could find you, and now you're asking me about my management company. I'm connecting dots and calling bullshit. What's really going on?"

"It's complicated," I say for the third time.

"That's life, I guess. Just be safe, okay?"

"I will. But before I go, can I just ask you…do you think your management company would be interested in merging with Bodega Talent?"

"I don't think so. Too volatile right now. But I'll check in with my manager and see what I can find out for you. And yes, for *sure* she'd take you on. Want me to ask?"

"That would be great. Thanks, Leila. I'll see you next week."

We cut the call, and I turn wide eyes toward Danny. "This is all my fault."

"This is one hundred percent not your fault," he says. "Your father got himself into this mess."

"That may be true. But I'm going to get him out of it."

Danny clears his throat. "How, exactly?"

I press my lips together. "To be honest, I'm not quite sure yet. Will you help me?"

He draws in a deep breath. "I don't know, Lex. I want to help *you*. But your father…"

"You just told me he confessed everything to you. That's a start, isn't it?"

He's quiet a long moment, and then he finally mutters, "I guess."

"There are two things that mean everything to him. His company and me. Did he do everything wrong? Absolutely. But I'm not going to turn on him now when he needs me the most."

"Are you forgetting what he just did to us?" he asks. He sits up a little. "And I don't just mean that he announced our wedding and my injury. I mean the fact that he stole everything from you."

"I'm not, and I'm not saying I forgive him. I'm not even saying I'd ever take him back as my agent once I cut ties. But what I *am* saying is that he's still my dad, and if I can help him, I will. Maybe he's done me dirty this time, but there have been plenty of times when he didn't."

He raises his brows. "You're a bigger person than me, then."

"Am I? Because as I recall, you went to the hospital earlier today to tell your father that you forgive him. Maybe I'm just taking a page from your book before it's too late."

He flattens his lips into a thin line.

"I know it's not what you want to hear, and you can say no. But, Danny, I'm going to ask you again. Will you help me bail my dad out and get back at Brooks all at the same time?" I ask.

He sucks in a long breath, and his eyes shift back to mine.

And then he nods. "Yeah. Okay. I'll do what I can to help. But I need you to make a promise to me."

"Anything," I breathe.

"The minute something feels off, we bail."

I nod. "The *second* something feels off, we bail," I say vehemently.

He leans in and presses his lips to mine, sealing our promise with a kiss.

Chapter 20
Danny

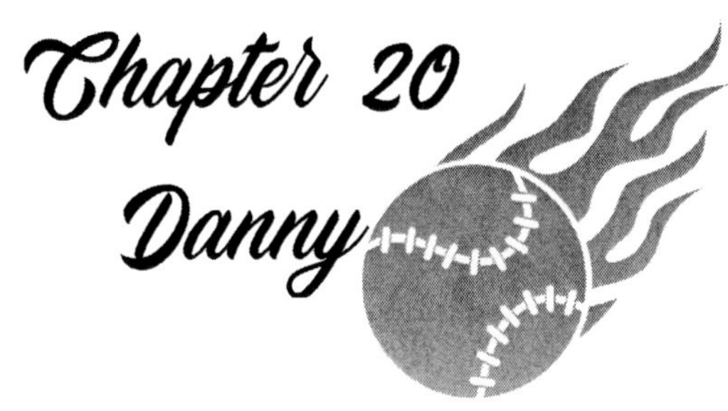

I don't exactly *like* the idea, but this is what my wife wanted.

And happy wife, happy life, right?

Or something along those lines.

I sit in the same chair I was sitting in not so long ago, this time casually with my ankle perched on the opposite knee. Alexis is in the chair beside me, facing off against her father.

She wanted me to take the helm on this conversation, but I'm sort of enjoying watching him squirm under her glare.

She's a force to be reckoned with, that's for damn sure.

"I know, Daddy," she begins.

Damn. I thought all that *Daddy* business was reserved for me.

Speaking of which…it's been far too long since I've fucked my wife. Maybe tonight. This goddamn wrist issue makes everything a little more difficult, but it's really only my cock I need for the main event. And her pussy. And tits. Maybe her ass.

"You know what?" he asks a little dumbly.

Come on, Raymond. You run a multi-million dollar business. Or, you did, anyway. Surely you can catch what she's throwing out there.

"I told her everything," I say pointedly. "She knows you needed the merger to save both her financial assets and your company. But we've discussed a solution."

"You've discussed a *what* now?" he asks.

"A solution," she says, enunciating the word carefully.

"You…you want to help me?" he asks.

"I do," she says, and she glances at me. "*We* do. Your success directly affects mine just as your prosperity does, and I want Bodega Talent Agency to rise from whatever this downfall is. I don't really understand everything that happened, but we're going to get you your company back and expose Brooks at the same time."

He shakes his head. "It's not that simple. We're out of cash. The only way to save us is a windfall, and nobody apart from D-Three is going to want to merge with a broken company."

"A merger is not the only way to save us," Alexis says quietly, and for someone who told me to lead the conversation before we came in here, she's sure as hell holding her own right now.

"What, a loan? No bank is going to invest in a failure," he says.

"The bank of Brewer will," I say flatly.

His eyes dart to mine as his brows shoot up in surprise. "What?" he breathes.

"You heard me."

"Why would you possibly help me after the way I've acted toward you?" he asks.

I fold my arms over my chest. "Because like it or not, for better or worse…you're my father-in-law now. My wife has a big stake in your success, and that means I do, too. And I will do anything for her."

His jaw slackens a little as if he can't actually believe I just said that, and then his gaze shifts to his daughter. "And you, my darling girl. Same question. Why are you helping me?"

She draws in a deep breath for strength, and I grab her hand and squeeze it. Her eyes meet mine, and she turns back toward her dad. "You probably don't remember this, but right before Mom died, back when she knew the end was coming, she told me to take care of you. I promised I would. And if I walked away from you now, if I let you suffer through this alone…well, I'd be breaking that promise."

He closes his eyes for a beat and draws in a deep breath, and then he leans back in his chair. He shakes his head a little. "She made me promise the same for you, and I'm afraid I broke my promise. I haven't taken care of you the way I should have. But you met someone who does, and for that…I'm pretty damn grateful." His eyes shift back to me. "I'm sorry for what I've done to you. I couldn't see beyond my own anger or beyond the hole I dug for myself. And you came in here ready to roll up your sleeves and help anyway, and even though it's shameful to even be in this situation, I can't tell you what that means to me."

"So you'll accept our help?" I ask.

He closes his eyes again as if it physically pains him to even consider it. "I don't think I have any other choice if I want to save the company."

I press my lips together. He's probably right.

"It might get uncomfortable," I say. "We'll need to take a look at your financials and sensitive information in order to get a business plan together. I have some people in mind I work with, and I called them earlier and explained what's going on. They're on board to help, but I need to gather some data to send over to get started right away."

"You called someone?" Raymond asks.

"I've got people." I lift a modest shoulder, but the truth is, I'm lucky to have a pretty wide network of friends. Only a select few know me well, like Cooper and Rush, and now Alexis, but I try not to do people dirty, and apart from a few women who got pissed I didn't want more than one night plus Alexis's dad, I don't make it a habit to get on people's bad sides.

He chuckles. "You're full of surprises."

"That's one of the things your daughter loves about me most."

She shrugs. "He's not wrong."

I'm about to joke about how she also likes the cock, but I realize it's definitely the wrong audience.

We'll just focus on taking one step at a time here.

"I don't want Brooks to know I'm not going through with the merger," he says quietly.

"Neither do we," I say.

"Oh," Alexis says. "And we'll need some quick cash, so I'll need you to focus on endorsements or gigs that work with my filming schedule so we can start to get above water. Danny's loan will help fund your other clients so nobody has to feel any sort of hit. We need you to just continue like it's business as usual."

"What's the catch?" he asks, suddenly a little tentative.

To be honest, that wasn't something Alexis and I discussed going into this conversation.

I know nothing about the music industry, but Alexis can teach me. She's a fucking expert if there ever was one.

I know a little about business. In fact, my undergraduate degree is in business. Even so, I do have my own career I'll need to attend to…but with a broken wrist, I have a little longer off-season than I was planning to have. I can help out with Bodega Talent and then rejoin my teammates once the medical staff clears me. And when my playing days are over, I'll have a career to fall back on if it's what I want. And if it isn't, then it's just a damn good investment. If I have people on top of Raymond and I have the right checks and balances in place, we'll be fine. He's already got the names and the clout on his roster. He got greedy, but he's lucky he has a daughter who cares an awful lot about him to get him back in the black.

"Fifty-one percent," I say.

"Fifty-one percent?" he scoffs. "No way."

I rise to my feet and shrug as if I don't care one way or the other, as if I'm going to walk out of the room now because the conversation is over. "Okay. Good luck with everything, then."

Alexis's jaw drops, and her voice is low when she speaks. "Danny, we didn't talk about that."

"You told me he planned to pass the company down to you someday." I lift a shoulder. "This is just expediting the process. And if you own the company, you own everything in it." I say the words meaningfully. I've thought this through. She wanted to ensure the safety of her masters, and this is just one way to do that. This gives her the control she never had but always deserved.

"You want *Alexis* to have fifty-one percent?" Raymond demands.

"I want *us* to have fifty-one percent," I clarify. "It'll be among the first of our marital assets. You can take it or leave it, Mr. Bodega, but if you leave it, your company is as good as dead."

He's quiet as his eyes study me, and eventually he says, "Let me think about it."

"Think as much as you want, but we need an answer by morning." My voice comes out harsher than I intend for it to, but we decided we're heading back to Vegas in the morning.

We have a house to close on there, another house to pack up and move out of, and I need to meet with the team doctor about my wrist. We'll need to be back here soon anyway for Alexis to resume filming, and I've been poking around looking at some places in Los Angeles that'll fit my budget plus have all the things Alexis wants while still saving enough to help invest in the agency.

"Okay," Raymond says.

"Okay…you'll let us know? Or okay…you agree to the terms?" Alexis clarifies.

He lets out a heavy sigh. "I agree to the terms." His voice is quiet and withdrawn, but a verbal agreement still counts.

A sense of relief filters through my chest. "I'll have my lawyer send over the paperwork."

And then I take my wife upstairs.

Chapter 27
Alexis

I let out a huge sigh of relief once we're back in my bedroom.

Danny grins as he looks at me, and then he locks the door.

He remains by the door, his eyes heating as they fall on me. "God, you're hot when you're negotiating."

I laugh. "Well, you're hot all the time."

"We're just two hot people standing in a bedroom with a large bed waiting to be used."

"Then use it," I say coyly, and he takes that as his cue. He stalks toward me, and my thighs seem to automatically clench at just the sight of him walking toward me.

This is all still so surreal. For one thing, I never thought I'd actually be having sex in this bedroom without a care in the world. But for another thing…he's my *husband*. I still can't quite believe that. It's like I'm living in some dream, and while things are falling down around me, he's there to pick up the pieces and make sure I'm okay as he dusts me off.

He's really an entire dream wrapped up into one fine man.

And it's not just all that.

The fact that I own fifty-one percent of Bodega Talent Agency means that *I own my masters*. I'm in control of my career for the first time in my life, and there's a gratifying feeling in that mixed with a new level of power I've never felt before.

"I love you," I say softly once he's standing a breath away.

"I love you, too."

"Thanks for having my back. For agreeing to do this. For…just being you."

"I just wanted you to have what's rightfully yours, Lex," he says softly. "And I want our kids to have it someday, too—if they want it."

My heart skips a beat at his words. "Our kids," I say softly.

He nods. "Think we should try for one sometime soon?"

"I want to enjoy my husband for a while first," I say. "But I don't think there's any harm in practicing."

"Oh, there's definitely no harm in practicing," he agrees, and his lips collide with mine.

Warmth starts in my core and spreads through me as thoughts of a long and happy future together flood through my mind. I shift so I'm as close to him as I can be, and he deepens our kiss as he thrusts his hips against mine.

I pull back for just a beat. "Are you okay to do this with a broken wrist?"

His eyes heat with lust. "I don't need my wrist for what I'm about to do to you." He grabs my chin with his good hand, slams his mouth back to mine, and then lets his hand trail down to my breast. He massages me there for a few beats, and then his hand trails down to my hip. "But I'm going to need your help."

"Anything," I breathe.

"Strip for me," he demands.

Dancing is second nature to me, so I turn him until his back is to the bed, and I gently push on his chest until he's perched on the edge of the mattress.

And then I start stripping for him as requested. I slowly unbutton my jeans as I dance, and then I slide them down my legs as I make eye contact with him, dragging my bottom lip between my teeth.

I dance around him and play with the hem of my shirt for a bit, lifting it and lowering it, teasing him before I tear it off and toss it to the ground.

I'm in a lace bra and panty set, and his breath hitches as he stares at me. He makes me feel like the sexiest woman in the world when he looks at me like that.

I move toward him and straddle his waist, gyrating over him as I give him a lap dance. Presumably he's had these before, and I don't have a ton of stripping experience, but the way he's breathing heavily as his cock gets harder and harder beneath me tells me that this is the lap dance of his dreams.

I take his jawline between my hands and lower my lips to his, our tongues immediately dancing together as he loops his good arm around me and holds me steady over him. I shift my hips over him, riding his cock with far too many clothes separating us, and I kiss him with urgency as my own desire builds. The ache inside is throbbing, but with every thrust of my hips against his cock, the friction brushes against my clit, pushing me higher and higher, closer and closer as the kiss turns downright brutal, our tongues locked in a battle that's beautiful and messy and perfect.

I slide along his cock again, wishing we were both naked as the sudden need for release screams through me, a fire ripping down my spine that's so intense I whimper into his mouth.

He groans as I slide over him again, and I don't know if he knows how close I am right now, but he pulls back. "I need to be inside you," he says.

I climb off him, eager to give him everything he needs, and I work his pants until they're off. I pull his shirt over his head, and then I strip out of my bra and panties, the pretense of dancing long gone as need and desire take hold.

I straddle him again, linking an arm around his neck as I grip his cock with my other hand. I slide down onto him as our eyes meet, a fiery heat traveling between us as a soft cry escapes my lips at the feel of him entering me.

"I love you," he murmurs softly, and my lips meet his parted ones as we start to move in perfect harmony together. I slide up and down his engorged cock, holding onto him as our bodies move in this way. He pushes up hard as I slide down at the same time, and the full feeling is pure heaven.

He breaks the kiss and angles his neck down to suck one of my nipples into his mouth, and I arch my back to push it more fully into his mouth.

"Oh my God," I cry.

He groans, the hum vibrating against my nipple, and he lets it out of his mouth long enough to say, "I want you to come all over my cock, Lex. I want you to scream my name while you're coming."

Oh. My. God. "Yes," I breathe. "Yes, yes, yes."

He starts to thrust a little harder as he sucks my nipple back into his mouth. "Touch your clit while you fuck me, baby," he says around my nipple, and the dirty talk alone is about to get me off.

I cry out as I slide my hand between us to touch myself, and he grunts when I slide my first and second fingers in a v-shape between us where we're connected so he can feel the extra grip on his cock. I reach down to touch his balls, and he growls as he lets go of my nipple.

"I'm gonna come," he says.

"So am I," I pant.

"Then touch that gorgeous clit and come for me."

"Oh my God, Danny!" I practically scream as the orgasm hits me *hard* the second I touch my clit.

"Fuck yes, Lex," he growls as the brutal climax hits us at the same time. He shoves into me as I rub my clit through the orgasm, and we ride the beautiful wave together.

I stay connected to him as we both come down from the high, and we pant in sync, breathing together as we somehow find ourselves bonding still closer together, as if every time we do this, we're a little more connected. And somehow, every time we do this, it gets better. I thought it was as good as it gets already, but he continues to surprise me in all the very best ways.

Eventually I climb off him, and we lie together in the afterglow before we force ourselves up to clean up and get ready for bed.

And then I fall asleep with a smile on my lips.

Chapter 22
Alexis

When I wake, it's a little after eight and Danny is still sleeping. I stretch as quietly as I can, and just as I'm about to slip out of bed, an arm comes around me and pulls me back until my back is flush with his front.

"Where the hell do you think you're going?" he demands, and I giggle.

"I'm ready to go back home."

"I thought this was home," he mutters.

"It was. But now home is where you are, and we need to get back to Vegas. We have to pack up and get over to our new house."

"I like the sound of that. *Our* new house," he repeats, and I have to admit, I like the sound of it myself.

"Then let's get to it," I say. "Time's a-wasting."

He chuckles as he thrusts his hips against my ass. "Well you know how much I hate to waste time."

"Danny! Again?"

"Babe, it will *always* be again. It will *never* be enough."

God, I love him.

After a quick morning romp and a shower, I help him pack up his stuff and we're ready to head *home* to Vegas.

I never consciously made the decision that I was relocating to Vegas, but apparently, I am.

He needs to be here for his job. I can make pretty much anywhere my home base.

I still want that home in San Diego, and I've given Gregory everything he needs to make it happen.

I'm not sure what made me think I needed to protect myself by creating a few of my own accounts that I slipped money into each month that would go untouched by my father, but I'm damn glad I did.

Maybe it was my mom speaking to my intuition and looking out for me.

Whatever the case, I have enough for the house.

But I don't have enough for the house *and* my next tour.

I might have enough to fund my next album, especially if I can get the equipment to self-produce. I've been around long enough to know how the process works, and I'm proficient on several instruments. I could do a lot of it myself and add the rest in post-production.

I have a lot of ideas for getting Bodega Talent out of the hole my father dug, and I can't wait to get in the car for our five-hour trip back home to discuss them all with Danny.

Especially since we own the majority of the company now.

It's ours, and it'll be a labor of love. Or, at least, it'll be a labor of ideas for now and putting the right people in the right places to see it soar again.

That's my hope, anyway. It's our shared vision.

Brooks hasn't been around much the last forty-eight hours, something I'm not exactly sad about. If we don't want him to know the merger isn't still on, then it's better I don't run into him. I may just slug him for taking advantage of my father the way he has.

And me.

He deserves a good slugging, that's for damn sure.

But I have a strong feeling he'll get his in the end.

Still, when we bid my father goodbye before slipping into the Yukon to head back to Vegas, I can't help but ask my dad, "Where's Brooks?"

We could fly instead of taking the Yukon, but this way we won't be hounded at the airport, and we'll get a little extra measure of privacy.

Plus, you know…road head. It's harder to do on a plane. Air head? Except I'll be driving, so that's out either way.

"He's spending time at his dad's house. Probably plotting how to take over the world," he says.

"Well, we'll be back by Tuesday night since filming resumes after the holiday. Take care of yourself until then, okay?" I say, folding myself into my dad for a hug.

"You take care of yourself, too. And that husband of yours," he says.

It makes my heart happy to hear the words—even happier that it's my dad speaking them, as if he's come to terms with the fact that it's real.

He turns to Danny. "And take care of my girl."

Danny nods. "I consider it my top priority."

My dad presses his lips together. "I know you do, and I can't tell you how much that means to me."

Hugs and kisses are issued, and then Danny and I take off.

We're less than ten minutes into the trip when he says, "So I have some ideas about Bodega."

"Oh my God, me too!" I say a little too enthusiastically.

He chuckles. "Can I just say that I love that we have a project to manage together?"

"So do I, actually. I wasn't expecting to go to my dad's asking about unfreezing my accounts and leaving a few days later as majority owner in his company, but here we are."

"What are your ideas?" he asks.

"You go first," I suggest.

He nods. "Well, I think you're our biggest asset here. We can attract new clients easily with your endorsement, and having you take on a bigger role with the agency will bring a fresh perspective. And you have a lot of friends in the industry. I don't think it would be hard to get them over to Bodega, especially if we offer attractive deals with lower commission rates."

"Totally agree. And I was also thinking we could expand our scouting department, and I could lure in local acts by taking the stage with them for a song or whatever," I suggest.

"Holy shit, that's a great idea. Imagine the crowd you'd bring in. Hell, imagine the excitement of the Bodegiacs waiting to see where you'll pop up next."

"And I need to leave D-Three, which we all know. Obviously not today since we're trying to do all this on the down low from Brooks. But I think we have a hole at Bodega when it comes to management, and I'm trying to figure out what to do. Maybe a management division," I suggest.

"I love that idea. But would that mean big spend?"

"Not if we can somehow lure in new clients for the agency also looking for a manager. It would pay for itself pretty quickly so long as the artist isn't a flop."

"And with your endorsement, they won't flop," he says.

I press my lips together and shake my head. "I could even bring them along as opening acts on the next tour."

"It would help offset a lot of costs if your openers didn't have to pay another management company," he says.

"Exactly."

"I think we're onto something. But again, I have no idea how any of this works, so we'll run it by my lawyer."

"I'd like to run everything by Gregory, too. He has a law degree, actually. He never took the bar, but he's one of the smartest people I know," I say.

"He has a law degree?" Danny repeats.

I nod. "Long story short, he got his degree while he was in the Army, but he was deployed before he could take the bar. And then his wife and daughter were killed, and he never took it."

"Does he want to?" he asks.

I shrug. "No idea. He's a man of few words, as you know."

He nods a little absently. "I feel like I'm learning something new about him every day."

"You are. How are things with him and your mom?"

He shrugs. "I've been a little busy with you and your dad, but things seem to be going well."

"Did you ever talk to him about the conversation you overheard?"

"I sent it to him," he admits. "We touched base briefly on it, but we haven't spoken since."

"Well, let's give him a call."

We do, and he answers right away. "Ms. Bodega, hello."

"Stop that Ms. Bodega nonsense. It's Alexis."

He chuckles. "Sorry. Hi, Alexis."

"And Danny," Danny says.

"Hello." He doesn't say *hi, how are you*, or mess around with any of the formalities of usual conversation.

"We're on our way back to Vegas and just wanted to give you a call with the latest," I begin, and then I proceed to word vomit all the details of everything that's happened over the last few days.

He's quiet when I finish, and I'm not sure if it's because he's waiting for me to add more or if he's processing everything I just said.

"Well?" I press.

"I'm happy to look over any contracts."

I laugh. "That's all you have to say?"

"I knew most of what you just told me. Danny filled me in. And I will be back on Tuesday evening to accompany you to the set."

"What's going on with Tracy?" I ask.

He's quiet for a beat, and then he says, "We're enjoying each other's company."

I grin at Danny, and he rolls his eyes a little, but I can tell he loves the idea of someone taking care of his sweet mother for a change.

"I love that for you," I say softly.

"I'm proud of you, Alexis," he says equally softly, and my heart squeezes.

"Thanks, Gregory."

"Hey Greg, take care of my mom, okay?" Danny says.

"Yes, sir."

He cuts the call, and we continue our trek toward Vegas, chatting about all the ideas we have for Bodega Talent Agency.

Chapter 23
Danny

When we get back to my place, we eat a quick lunch before we start the process of finding a moving company. I'd love to do it all myself, but with this wrist, I just can't.

And so we find a place that'll do it on short notice—for the right price, of course. They'll be here in two days to pack up this entire house and move it to the new house. And rather than worry about furniture, we hire an interior designer who's going to fill it with all the things we want after taking a quick inventory of our likes and dislikes, most of which happen to be on the same page.

I call the medical staff to get on the schedule for tomorrow, and I call Troy to let him know I'm in town and I'm meeting with the team doctors. He tells me he'll be there, and knowing I have his support means a whole lot.

Like Alexis has Gregory, I have Troy, and having someone who cares about our well-being in that paternal position means a whole hell of a lot given the ups and downs we've had with our own fathers.

And then we call our friends. Cooper and Gabby are free, and so are Rush and Anna, so we invite them over to our place for dinner.

Rush and Anna show up first, and Anna is absolutely *beaming* when she walks in.

She can't contain her excitement as she throws her hand out before she even greets us to show us the ring Rush gave her for Christmas in person rather than over a video chat.

"Congratulations!" Alexis squeals, and I give Rush a bro hug while the ladies squeal together and embrace.

I hug my sister next, and I murmur close to her, "You're good?"

"Never been better," she murmurs back, and I truly believe her.

Holy shit, this thing has certainly progressed while I've been tied up doing my own thing with Lex. "Where are the kids?" I ask.

"With Rush's mom," Anna says.

"So it's a whole family thing already?"

"We're here together, aren't we?" she points out.

I grin. "Never thought I'd see the day I'd be okay with a teammate marrying my sister, but here we are."

"Here we are," she agrees.

Cooper and Gabby arrive as we're standing in the foyer talking, and more hugs and congratulatory wishes are issued as Anna and Rush tell them their big news.

"Have you picked a date yet?" Alexis asks as we make our way into the kitchen as a big group, and if I had to guess who out of the three of us men here would be getting married first, I wouldn't have ever put myself at the top of the list.

Yet here we are.

"We're in no rush," Anna says, glancing over at Rush with a smirk. "My divorce has only been finalized for like five minutes, but we're looking at next year in the off-season. Maybe around Christmastime."

"So I was first, Cooper's next a month from now, and then you're up a year from now?" I ask.

"Sounds about right," Cooper says. "And we had the first kid, so someone else is up next."

Laughs are issued all around, but my sister corrects him. "I actually have two, so I think Danny and Alexis are next."

My face blanches as Alexis shrugs, and Cooper and Rush both laugh nearly hysterical laughs at the look on my face.

"No harm in trying, right?" Alexis deadpans.

"Like…right now?" I say dumbly.

"Maybe after everyone leaves."

I lean in toward her. "Definitely after everyone leaves."

My sister rolls her eyes.

Dinner arrives and we sit around the table laughing and eating, and we talk about playing poker, but I need both hands for that, so we opt for charades instead.

There's drinks and laughter, and there's even a little help with packing up a box or two before our friends head home.

And then I make good on that promise from earlier.

I meet with the team doctor the next morning, and he confirms it's a clean break. No nerve damage, no ligament damage. Thank God. So it really is just a waiting game on the progress to let the bone heal. He fits me for a splint and sends me on my way, instructing me to restrict movement as much as possible to allow for healing.

We close on the new place and get our keys on New Year's Eve, and we head over to our house, where I fuck my wife on the kitchen counter before we pop a bottle of champagne and celebrate the many blessings that have come our way over the last year.

What a year it's been.

Meeting Alexis Bodega.

Falling in love.

Winning the World Series.

Getting married.

And now…this.

This happiness. This bliss. This feeling like together, we can conquer anything that comes our way.

Her dad threatened to ruin me, and he even tried to make me believe the threat by outing our marriage and my injury in the same statement.

But it didn't touch what we have.

The only way he could ever really ruin me is if he somehow made Alexis believe his lies about me, but her faith in me is strong, and what we have is unbreakable.

My dad threatened to ruin me, too—to ruin *us*. But he didn't come close to touching us, either, despite his best efforts.

We had the right people on our side at the right time, and for that, I'll be forever grateful.

But most of all, I'm grateful for Alexis Bodega. The future may hold more storms—stronger ones than the ones we've already weathered, even. But if those didn't break us apart, the future ones won't, either.

If anything, they'll push us closer together. They'll force us to cling to one another, and I for one will never let go.

We don't get to move into the new place just yet because we have to head back to Los Angeles for Alexis to resume filming on Wednesday. But the next time we come back to Vegas, we'll be staying in our new home.

I can't wait.

As we approach the exit we need to take to head toward her dad's place, I glance over at her. "Don't you need to be in the right lane?"

"Oh…shit," she murmurs as we fly by the exit.

Do I sense…*sarcasm* in her tone?

"Listen up, backseat driver," she says. "Why don't you let me worry about where I need to be?"

I chuckle. "Yes ma'am."

She drives another few miles before she starts to merge over to the right, and eventually she takes an exit toward Hollywood Hills. She winds through some side streets up toward a gated community, and she punches in the gate code. We navigate a couple minutes through the neighborhood until she parks the car in the driveway of a mansion on the hillside.

Gregory stands in the driveway…with my mother.

I glance over at Alexis. "What did you do?"

Her eyes twinkle a little. "Remember how I said I hid a few accounts from my dad?"

I nod slowly.

"Well, I hid enough to afford this place. Welcome home."

My jaw slackens. "Has anyone ever told you how incredible you are?"

"Not in the last hour."

"Well, you're pretty fucking incredible, Alexis Bodega," I breathe.

"As are you, my dear husband." She grins at me, and it's the smile that's an immediate signal to my cock.

But since my mother is here, I put the skids on that idea.

For now.

The house is up on a hill overlooking downtown Los Angeles in the distance, and it's private and quiet up here. And one of the features I loved most about it is the separate guest house on the property—a nice place in its own right with two thousand square feet, two bedrooms, and two bathrooms located across the expansive pool from our side of the house.

Which means that even though Gregory and Danny's mom are here, we still get privacy for our first night in our new home.

And we're definitely going to need that. *Lots* of privacy…wink, wink.

The house came furnished, which was a blessing in disguise since we simply don't have the time to furnish it ourselves right now. Gregory managed a cleaning crew who came through to make it sparkle, and he and Tracy went through the place and took down anything they thought didn't fit our style.

And as I asked them to do that, I couldn't help but feel like we really hit the jackpot with the two of them. They were eager to help in any way they could, and the look of pure and utter shock on Danny's face tells me it was totally worth it.

Was it frivolous to spend this exorbitant amount of money on a mansion when I just bought a house in San Diego and I have serious financial woes thanks to my father?

Absolutely.

But Danny and I needed a home here in LA, and my need for a little separation from my father outweighed my fears about money.

I'll take on a few extra gigs. I can set my own price for private performances, something that was already high. Maybe it's time to raise it. And I'll do a few more sponsorships. We'll figure it out, and we'll be okay…all from the luxury of the dream house we own.

After we get out of the car and hug Tracy and Gregory, I ask Danny if he's ready for a tour of our new home. The first thing I see when I walk into the foyer is an enormous framed painting of the two of us at our wedding.

I turn around and see Tracy and Gregory standing behind us, both of them smiling.

"We couldn't let you move into your new home without a few personal touches," Tracy says.

I rush over to hug her, and she squeezes me tightly.

We wander aimlessly through the house, and while I'm used to living in luxury, there's something really special about the fact that we're able to live here because I do what I love for a living.

I realize I'm one of the lucky few. I'm incredibly blessed, and despite my father's best efforts to spend all my money, at twenty-eight, I'm still well off enough that I could retire if I wanted to.

I don't want to.

But I *do* want to slow down a little.

I do want to make some plans for my future with Danny.

Even though it was right for us, we were married quickly. Marriages are complicated and intricate, and while we're still very much in our honeymoon phase, this is also the time when we need to put in the work.

We can surprise each other with homes, but once the excitement and the newness wear off, where will we be?

I want to be in a stable relationship with the person I most love in the entire world. It'll be hard when he's traveling and I'm traveling, and so building that stable foundation now is essential.

And I have some plans for what comes next.

The album is already in the works, and I also have a plan to turn the movie and media room in this house into my own studio since it's already soundproofed. But beyond the goals that were already in place for this year, I have some ideas for where I want to take my career next.

And I can't wait to set the plans in motion so I can surprise my husband.

It'll be a way for us to have *time* together so we can build all the things we want for our future. Kids. A home. Family. Love.

We wander through the six bedrooms and eight bathrooms in this seven thousand square foot home plus the two thousand square foot guesthouse as all these thoughts race through my mind. We sit by the pool in the oasis of a backyard, my mind calming just from being out here in the fresh air surrounded by palm trees.

Gregory heads out to pick up dinner for us, and the four of us sit in our new kitchen around our new table as we pass around salad and chicken and vegetables.

"So what's going on with you two?" Danny asks bluntly as he takes another scoop of veggies.

I nearly choke on my chicken, but Tracy and Gregory handle it with grace.

They glance at each other as if they knew this question was coming, and then Tracy fields it.

"We've spent the last week together, and we're really enjoying each other's company," she says.

Gregory laughs. He *laughs.* He'll sort of chuckle every now and again, but hearing laughter is a rare occurrence from the man who rarely shows any emotion at all. "You could say that. We're just two old people who found each other at the right time."

"Speak for yourself, G," Tracy scolds as she thins her lips to shoot him a glare.

He laughs again. *Again*. I'm flabbergasted by the whole thing, but I guess that's what love does to someone.

And if anyone deserves to find love, it's these two.

They've teamed up to help the two of us, and somehow they found everything neither one of them was ever looking for.

My heart feels full and happy as I sit around this table with these people who have come to mean so very much to me.

I still have my father, and we'll work on mending our relationship. But this right here is the found family I've been searching for my entire life.

My hot and sexy husband. My wonderful mother-in-law. And my security guard turned pseudo-father.

It doesn't get much more special than that.

Chapter 25
Alexis

I could live in this bliss forever, but unfortunately, that's not an option. I have to return to set on Wednesday morning bright and early, and Danny set an alarm to ensure I wake up and get out the door on time.

And waiting down in my brand-new kitchen for me after I take a quick shower and throw on some sweats is Gregory.

"You ready?" he asks.

I rush over to give him a big hug. "I'm so glad you're here."

"Feels good to get back to work, doesn't it?" he murmurs.

For as chaotic and crazy as the last couple weeks have been, the routine of having Gregory here as we get ready to head into work feels nothing short of absolutely normal. Though I have to admit, I'm ready for filming to wrap on this one. I thought my heart was in acting, but the more time I've spent thinking about it, the more I know it's in music. I think I was leaning away from music and leaning into acting so hard because my father is so connected to my musical career.

But I knew it was time for a change.

And I'm thinking that change comes in taking control of my career.

Now that I've cleared the air with my father and we've started on the right track of getting the agency profitable again without the merger, I'm ready to start working with a new agent. I want to redesign my representation so that I have a management team who will handle tours, endorsements, and overall strategies, along with a team of publicists to handle my appearances and the media. It's a little different than a traditional agent like my father has been my whole career, but since I'm at a place where I'm taking over for a lot of what we've done my whole career, I am ready to make a big change in how my team works.

Instead of an agent and a manager who run everything, I'm the boss. I'm in charge. I will pay an agent to help me strategize. I will pay a management team to help me achieve my goals. I will pay a publicist to take care of my image instead of having my father run that for me.

And my team will be entirely made up of women. Badass boss ladies ready to level up in their careers.

After work today, I am heading over to the Bodega offices to have a chat with some of the agents there. It's been a while since I've gone into the office at all since I live with my agent, but I know my father has some recommendations, and furthermore, I know that Danny will be there all day with the business associates he has flown in along with his lawyer to start the process of turning Bodega Talent around.

The other reason I want to be at the office tonight is because my father has called a late conference meeting where Brooks will be in attendance. At this meeting, he plans to let the company know that there's going to be a change in ownership, that Danny and I are now the majority stakeholders and that we will no longer be going through with the merger that was planned.

And I sure as hell am not going to miss the look on Brooks's face when he realizes D-Three and Bodega are no longer merging. It feels like the perfect way to start the year, and it also feels like the perfect way to issue a big, well-deserved *fuck you* to Brooks.

When I arrive on set, Leila is already there, and she pulls me into a big hug as soon as I walk into hair and makeup.

"Happy New Year," she says.

"Happy New Year," I repeat. "Did you do anything fun to celebrate?"

"I attended a charity event that was fancy-schmancy. How about you?"

"Danny and I had a quiet night in. It was a welcome change from the fancy-schmancy events I've attended for the last twelve years."

"Was that Gregory I saw dropping you off this morning?" she asks.

I nod. "A lot changed over our little break, but some things remained the same," I admit.

"What changed?" she asks.

I can't help a laugh.

"I filled you in on some of it, but…" I pause and shake my head, and then I launch into everything that's gone down. By the time I'm done talking, my hair and makeup are done, and everyone in the room knows the whole story. Thank goodness for those NDAs, though by the end of the day today, the only person I don't want to find out ahead of time will know anyway.

"I talked to my manager, and she is absolutely thrilled that you're interested. She wanted to set up a meeting with you to get the ball rolling as soon as possible," she says.

"I'm down for that," I say. "How does lunch today sound?"

Leila laughs. "I have no idea, but I'll get a call into her and ask. I just have one request."

"What?" I ask.

"Don't take all her attention away from me. I need her." She's begging me.

I laugh. "Well, maybe she has a recommendation of someone else at her firm who would be willing to represent me then."

The truth of the matter is I probably need multiple managers because there are multiple facets to what I do. But the other truth of it is I don't really want to pursue acting anymore. If a small role comes along and it fits, then I'll jump at it. But I don't want to leave music to go into acting when acting is one of the things that will pull me further away from Danny.

I'm not making decisions for my career one hundred percent based on Danny. But I am making decisions one hundred percent based on what's going to make me the happiest. And thinking thoroughly through all of this over the last two weeks, I know exactly what I want to do.

But I don't want to discuss that with Leila. I haven't even discussed it with Danny yet, though I am willing to talk to my management team about it ahead of filling him in just to ensure my idea is really going to be something that's going to work.

As it turns out, Leila's manager is available at lunchtime, and there's a knock at my door as I am digging into a salad. I assume it's either Danny or Gregory, so I yell *come in* from my seat on the couch.

When the door opens, a beautiful blonde woman about my age steps in. "Alexis Bodega," she says with a wide smile. "It's lovely to meet you. I'm Gemma Murphy from Roadrunner Management, and I'm ready to take on the world with you."

She's confident and sophisticated as she reaches out a hand to shake mine, and her grip is firm as her gaze is steady on mine.

I like her already.

She's exactly the kind of badass boss I want on my team.

"I'm so happy to meet you. Tell me all about Roadrunner and what you envision for the two of us," I say as I shove another forkful of lettuce into my mouth.

She launches into her spiel, and she sells me in the first ten seconds.

I love her already, and she came highly recommended. What's the worst thing that happens? We sign a contract for a year, and if it doesn't work out, we go our separate ways.

But what's the best thing that happens?

Well…then we take on the world together, just like she said.

Chapter 26

Danny

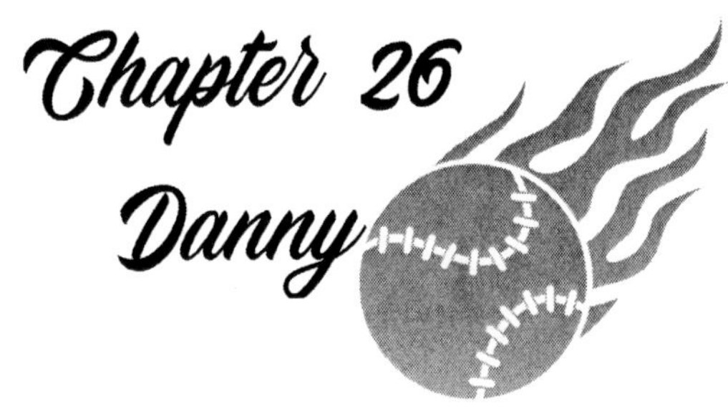

It doesn't quite feel real that this is mine.

I walk over to the windows and allow myself to look out over downtown Los Angeles, where Bodega Talent Agency is located. Maybe we could cut costs by moving the office, but deep down I know that's not the right answer. A big part of successfully running a place like this is reputation, and the best of the best work in offices that appear to be the best of the best.

We've gotten a lot done today and we have a solid plan to move forward to save this company. I know exactly how much money I'm investing, but I also know based on history that I'll get it all back tenfold. I think even Raymond is surprised at my business sense, and I have my mother to thank for that.

If it were up to me, I would've skipped college and gone straight to playing ball out of high school, but with her background in education, she encouraged me to think about what my future would hold after the game.

I glance down at my wrist and realize how right she was to do that. A centimeter to the right or left could've sent me in a completely different direction where I might not even get to play this year or the year after that or beyond.

All it takes is one wrong move and we could be out of the game completely. I don't prefer to think about that, but it is a harsh reality that I've seen happen on more than one occasion. Hell, it even happened to my best friend long before we were on the Vegas Heat together.

Cooper sustained an elbow injury that needed surgery, and he decided to call it quits. It was Troy who lured him back into the game once his injury was fully healed, and he helped lead our team to the victory we just had in the World Series.

I'm thankful for my clean break. I'm thankful all I will miss is a couple of games. It could've been a hell of a lot worse, and I'm lucky it wasn't.

"Thanks for all your work today, Danny," Raymond says, interrupting my thoughts. "I badly misjudged you, and for that, I am sorry."

"I appreciate that, Raymond." My voice is low and sincere. "I get it, man. You were backed into a corner, and you were trying to protect Alexis. I'm only operating from the same place."

"I see that now. You have an incredible instinct for this, and I'm thankful for all you're doing to save my company." He pauses, and then he tilts his head thoughtfully as he stares at me. "*Our* company," he amends.

"I'm glad I'm in a position to be able to help."

"Are you ready for this meeting?" he asks, and just as he poses the question, the conference room door opens, and my entire reason for being here walks in.

When I say *my entire reason for being here*, I don't just mean here in this conference room or even in this office. I mean this world. This life.

My wife.

We stare across the room at each other for a beat, almost as if neither of us can really believe our luck that we're both here in the same place, that we're really truly married. That this is our life now. She walks across the room toward me, and my lips curl into a smile at the sight of her. I take her into my arms when she gets to me and press a small kiss to her lips.

"How was your first day back on set?" I ask.

"It was good," she says. There's a twinkle in her eye that tells me there's more to it but that she isn't ready to reveal what it is just yet. It's these little moments where I love what our relationship is growing into the most—that unspoken kind of communication where we don't have to say anything in order to say everything.

"How did things go here?" she asks.

"Great," Raymond says. "We have a plan, and we have the right people getting placed into the right places, and we know that it may take some time to move to where we want to be, but we're ready to move into the next phase of Bodega Talent Agency."

"And we can't wait to stick it to that asshole Brooks," I add.

Alexis laughs. "Does he have any idea what's coming?"

Her dad shakes his head.

"What do you say we have a little fun with him, then?" she suggests.

Her dad narrows his eyes at her. "What kind of fun are you thinking?"

"Oh, I don't know." She taps her chin. "Maybe the kind of fun where we lead him to think that we've been working all day on this merger, and then we kick him in the nuts."

I laugh as her dad's jaw drops clean down to the floor.

"I can't believe you just said that," he breathes.

"Oh, Dad," she says, shaking her head a little. "I keep telling you I'm not a little girl anymore."

He walks over and slings his arm around her shoulders. "No, I suppose you're not," he says, and he squeezes her into his side a little. "And I know you stopped by to talk to some of the different agents here, and I want to give a hearty endorsement for Evan Thompson."

"I appreciate the recommendation, Dad, but I'd like to have a chat with all of the female agents on your staff. I've worked with men my entire career, and I am ready to take things in a new direction. I think women will understand my vision in a different way than men."

He opens his mouth to protest, but when he sees the stern look on his daughter's face, he clamps his mouth shut tight. "Of course, Alexis."

Well color me shocked. I didn't think people could change, but here stands Raymond proving me way the fuck wrong.

And it's the kind of wrong I'd love to be proven over and over again.

"If you'll excuse me, I have some agents to interview," Alexis says. "What time is the meeting?"

"About thirty minutes," Raymond says. "Certainly you'll need more ti—"

Alexis holds up a hand as she shakes her head. "I'll know. I haven't been allowed to give my intuition much chance to shine, but all that changes starting right now."

Her dad closes his mouth and presses his lips together for a beat, and then he nods. "Right. Okay, then. I can reserve a conference room and let you know who's still around."

"Anyone not around isn't working hard enough," she says with a tight smile.

She's got a point. It's only four-thirty. Working hours go until five, but in the agency business, there's always work to be done.

She wants someone who's already dedicated to their job, and I don't blame her.

You don't get to the level Alexis Bodega's at without a whole lot of intelligence.

Her dad may have silenced her for a long time, but she can handle herself. I believe in her, and she believes in herself. That's all we need.

She excuses herself to the conference room her dad reserved for her, and we go over a few more details. And then it's time for the stakeholder meeting.

Brooks shows up punctually at five along with his father, and the officers and directors of Bodega are already gathered. Brooks and his father are the only two in the room who don't quite know what's coming yet. Alexis rushes in at five-oh-one.

"Sorry I'm late," she pants.

"Was your meeting successful?" I ask.

She grins and nods as she slides into the open seat beside me.

"What are Alexis and Brewer doing here?" Brooks asks. "Isn't this a meeting about the merger?"

Raymond opens his mouth to talk, but Alexis beats him to it.

"Oh yes, it sure is," she says. "And as much as I wanted to beat around the bush and lead you in one direction, I think it'll be even more fun just to come out with it. We're not merging."

She says it flatly.

"Excuse me?" Brooks asks.

"Bodega Talent Agency is not merging with D-Three," Raymond says, enunciating each word as if Brooks just didn't hear it right the first time.

"Like hell you're not," Brooks says. "What about the money?"

Raymond shakes his head a little. "Alexis and Danny know everything, as do all the others in this room."

"What is *everything*, exactly?" Arthur asks, looking extremely confused as he glances between his son and his would-be partner.

"Brooks blackmailed me into merging with D-Three. He wanted a piece of Alexis, and he weaseled his way into very nearly getting her to marry him," Raymond says.

Arthur looks well and truly shocked. "Brooks…is this…is this *true*?"

Brooks looks guilty, and he doesn't have to say a word at all. He slumps back in his chair like a petulant teenager, and it's quite a bit more gratifying to see him like that than I was expecting.

"I'm afraid it is," I offer quietly. "Alexis and I have bought fifty-one percent of Bodega, and we no longer want to go through with this merger. We have enough resources to get Bodega back into the black."

"You can't just stop a merger," Arthur says. "There are legalities—"

"We're well aware of the legalities, Mr. Donovan, and our legal team has taken a hard look at all of it," I say. "We were able to jump over some hurdles thanks to your son's agenda to marry Alexis paired with the timing of the holidays, and legally we can pull the plug on this whole thing."

"But you can't sign over the company to somebody else," Arthur points out.

"Actually, in the case of bankruptcy, we can," Raymond says.

"*Bankruptcy*?" Arthur breathes.

I nod. "Raymond filed chapter eleven, and part of the restructuring agreement is having his daughter and her husband take the helm of this company. Thank you for your interest in Bodega, but we'll be proceeding on our own without the merger."

I wish I could take a photo of Brooks to look back on with glee, but I refrain.

I have a feeling Arthur is going to make that asshole pay, and pulling the merger he was so intent on is just the first step in our revenge plan.

Karma will take care of the rest, and that's good enough for me.

"Oh, and you need to get the fuck out of my house. Immediately," Raymond says.

Brooks sinks further down into his chair.

He's finally getting what he deserves, and I couldn't be happier about that.

Chapter 27
Alexis

"We need to go public with this," I say quietly.

The meeting is over, and everyone has cleared out of the conference room. I swear, I thought Arthur was going to drag Brooks out by his ear. He was positively fuming over what his son did, and it was such a delight to witness.

But it's not enough. He needs to go down, and I'm brainstorming all the possibilities of how to go about doing it. Now that we've confronted Brooks and what we know, we need to save the reputation of this company.

I've chosen my new manager. I've chosen my new agent at the agency I now own.

I'm finally in control.

"I agree," my dad says. "But first…"

He tosses a manila folder across the table toward me, and I flip open the cover.

I read the top line and my eyes meet my father's.

He presses his lips together and nods. “I figured you’d want to take care of shredding it.”

A small smile lifts my lips. “I may hold onto it as a souvenir of my first contract.”

He chuckles a little. “Alexis, you’ve more than proven that you’re capable of handling yourself and your career. I’m so sorry for the way I’ve acted all these years.”

I shake my head. “Don’t be sorry, Daddy. We move forward now. We’ve had a lot of success together, and you’re still a forty-nine percent owner of this agency. You’re still very much a part of my career, and I want you to be because you’re the best at what you do…but now I’m in control.”

“I appreciate you saying that. I’ll be as much or as little a part of things as you want. I guess it took losing both my daughter and my company to realize how terribly I’ve treated you. But all that changes now,” he promises.

I hope he holds true to that promise. I think he will.

“So how do we want to handle going public?” Danny asks.

“I have an idea,” I say.

Both my dad and Danny look over at me, and it feels really good to have them on the same page now. It took a whole lot to get here, but now that we’re here, I can’t help but feel like everything is working out just like it was always supposed to.

“I haven’t addressed anything over the last month, and I think it’s time. I have a lot I want to say, and I think I’m ready for an exclusive,” I say.

“An exclusive?” my dad asks. “With who?”

“I have someone in mind, but she’s in Vegas. She’s primarily a sports reporter, but she had me on her podcast a few months ago, and the way she handled the tough questions made me feel comfortable enough to open up,” I say.

“Are you talking about Jolene Nash?” Danny asks.

I nod. “She’s married to the coach of the Vegas Aces and they run a podcast together. She’d be perfect. She used to be a team correspondent, so she's used to the cameras, and I loved her when we talked."

"And it would bolster her career a few notches to interview you," my dad finishes.

I shrug. "It won't hurt it."

"You'll be putting her on the map, darling. Are you sure you want to do that? You don't want to aim higher? Say…Oprah?" he presses.

"She's already on the map, Dad. And I want her to ask the hard-hitting questions the others would be afraid to. I'm ready to tell all, including why I didn't marry Brooks and why Bodega isn't merging with D-Three." I nod my head emphatically at the end of my speech.

"Okay, then. Let's put in a call to Jo—"

I hold up a hand to cut him off. "Charlotte is handling it."

"Charlotte?" my dad repeats.

"My new agent," I clarify. It's her first job as my new agent, and it's a trial run to see if she can get me exactly what I've asked for.

She's working hand-in-hand with Gemma, my new manager, and it's a test of sorts for both of them.

Danny's lawyer—*my* lawyer, now—is working up a contract for both of these women, and I'm thrilled to be working with them.

I can't wait to see what the future holds.

There's a knock at the conference room door, and when my father yells at whoever it is to come in, Charlotte stands there. "Mrs. Brewer, I have your interview scheduled with Jolene Nash this Saturday at noon at her home studio in Las Vegas. I've given her a list of talking points, and she will send you the list of questions by tomorrow evening." She looks triumphant, and she should. She rocked it.

"Thank you, Charlotte." I beam at her. "Well done."

She offers me a smile.

"You're hired, by the way," I say, and her smile turns into a wide grin.

"Thank you so much, Alexis! I promise I won't let you down." She's squealing a little, and I feel the excitement, too.

"I know you won't," I say simply. I stand, walk over to her, and give her a hug. "Now go celebrate. We've got an exciting future ahead of us, and I'm going to keep you very, very busy."

She squeezes me back, and then she heads out.

"You stole my best agent," my dad whines, and I laugh.

"I'm putting your best agent to work," I correct. "You better get started on redistributing the rest of her clients because I'm going to need her all to myself."

He chuckles as we wrap things up, and I return to filming for the two days that follow. And then I find myself in Vegas at the new house I'm sharing with my husband the night before my interview with Jolene.

"Are you nervous?" Danny asks me.

I shake my head. "I'm excited. I can't wait to get the truth out there. I can't wait to tell the world how I fell for you. Are *you* nervous?"

"Maybe a little," he admits. "But nothing changes. We're already being followed everywhere we go. This just puts the truth out there so we can live our lives without other people making assumptions about us."

I kiss my husband then sleep well despite the big interview I have coming up.

Danny makes me bacon and eggs for breakfast, and a small team of stylists comes by to prep me for the interview.

And then it's time. He drives me over to Jolene's house, a mansion not far from where we live, and she greets me at the door with a smile. A little boy around seven or eight stands behind her, and his eyes are wide.

"It really is Alexis Bodega!" he murmurs in awe.

"It really is," I say. "What's your name?"

"Jonah."

"Well, Jonah, it's lovely to meet you. Did you know your mom is amazing?" I ask him, and I wink at Jolene.

"Yeah, she's pretty cool." He shrugs a little, and then Jolene welcomes us in.

"It's so nice to finally meet you in person," she says, holding out a hand to shake mine.

"And you," I say.

"Right this way," she says, leading us toward her studio. "Danny, will you get on camera, too? Usually we're more football-focused, but I've interviewed Troy a few times and I know a thing or two about baseball."

Danny chuckles. "This is Alexis's interview."

"And I'll be talking about you, so yes, he'll be on, too."

"But I didn't even shave!" he protests.

I roll my eyes. "You never shave." I reach over and finger his scruff. "And you know I like it that way."

Jolene giggles. "You two are adorable."

"Brewer!" a voice behind us says.

"Nash!" Danny says, greeting the head coach of the Vegas Aces football team, Lincoln Nash. They do some kind of bro handshake. "Good to see you again, man. I didn't know if you'd be here."

"I've got to get to practice, but I'm glad I ran into you," Lincoln says. "We have our annual charity ball coming up, and we'd love to highlight some of our favorite ballplayers in town. Interested?"

Danny nods. "I'd love to take part."

"I'll have our charity director get in touch with you," he says. "And if you're up for it, we're doing a local cornhole game for charity the week before the Super Bowl."

"I'm up for it. Definitely. And Coach?" Danny says.

Lincoln looks at him expectantly.

"Kick the Bears' ass this weekend, okay?"

Lincoln grins. "You got it, man." He walks over and gives Jolene a kiss. "You got this." He murmurs the words, but I don't miss them.

"She's definitely got this. When I first had this idea, I knew I needed the best in the business. And here we are," I say.

Jolene blushes, and then we get set up in her studio. She introduces me to Dave, the camera operator in the corner, and has me take a seat in a beautiful leather chair. Beside me is a little table with a cozy winter set-up complete with a blanket and candles, and it's a calm and relaxing atmosphere to do this.

"You ready?" Jolene asks.

I nod emphatically. "Ready."

Chapter 28
Alexis

"Alexis, thank you so much for joining me today. I'd like to start at the beginning. Why did you decide not to marry your manager, Brooks Donovan?" Jolene begins.

"It never felt right to marry Brooks," I begin. "It's complicated, but my father who was also my agent carefully crafted my image to look a certain way. I always believed it was because he was trying to protect me, and he was. But he was also protecting his own interests with the company, and it mostly had to do with money." I tread carefully since I don't want my dad to come out of this looking bad…even though he did behave badly. I still want to protect him to some degree. "When the media linked Brooks and me together four years ago, we didn't bother correcting them. And the next natural step was marriage, right? My dad and Brooks made all these plans for this huge wedding, but in the meantime, I'd met someone and I'd fallen in love. If not for that, I might've actually gone through with the wedding."

"Can you take us back to the moment when you made the decision to run out on your own wedding?" Jolene asks.

"I felt this immense pressure the entire day. I needed to make a choice, and I should've done it far sooner. I knew the man I loved was a mere twenty minutes away, and I knew my father and Brooks and all the guests were waiting for me to walk down the aisle. My security guard, Gregory—he was going to walk me down the aisle, and he told me it was time. I looked toward the exit, and I looked at the door that would take me down the aisle, and I knew in my heart there was only one right choice. I took Gregory's keys and bolted."

"And you ran to Danny Brewer?" she asks.

I nod. "Yes. Danny and I met at the Vegas Heat stadium on opening day when I was there to sing a few songs. We slowly got to know each other as I toured across America and he played an entire season that ended with him winning the World Series. Over that time, I fell in love with him, and I knew he was the man I was destined to end up with. I couldn't marry Brooks when my heart was with Danny."

"Rumor has it you married Danny. Did you marry him so you wouldn't have to marry Brooks?" Jolene presses.

This is why I wanted *her* to interview me. Others might've been scared to ask that question, but I want the truth to be known.

I shake my head. "Initially, Danny offered that as an option. But when we decided to go through with it, we did it purely out of love. It was Danny and me, Gregory, and Danny's mom. That's it. She officiated. Gregory walked me to Danny. It was small and intimate, and that's how I knew it was perfect. It wasn't a lavish affair with hundreds of guests. It wasn't a gaudy diamond that didn't fit my style. It was just about the two of us and our love, and I will never forget what a beautiful moment it was."

"So your father didn't know?"

I shake my head. "He didn't find out until Christmas Eve when I had to be back in Los Angeles for the live special."

Jolene nods. "How did he feel about that, and what's your relationship like with your dad now?"

"I'll start by saying we're on great terms now. But he wasn't happy when he found out." I go on to explain how Brooks was holding something over him. I even go so far as to say he was being blackmailed. It's a criminal offense in California, and at this point, I feel like Brooks should pay for what he's done.

I don't hold back when I tell her about D3 and how Brooks was plotting right under his father's nose the whole time. I tell the truth about how I felt like a prisoner in my own home until I took control of my life. And I'm honest about how it was falling in love with Danny that opened all the doors to all of it.

He made me see my own worth, and it was only with his support and encouragement that I landed in the position where I am now.

"What a comeback story," Jolene says. "So what's next for you, Alexis? More movies? More music?"

I glance up at Danny.

He doesn't know about my plan yet, but Charlotte and Gemma have been working around the clock to make this happen over the last few days, and this morning before I came here to this interview, I signed on the dotted line.

His brows dip as if he can read on my face that I'm about to say something that even he doesn't know about.

"I'll finish filming *Break Free* by the end of the month. Then I'm going to take some time with my husband before he has to report for the season, and I'll work on my next album in the spring," I say, not giving away my big reveal just yet.

"Any hints as to what's coming on the new album? Will your recent experiences be reflected in your music?" she asks.

I nod. "I've been writing new songs all through falling in love with Danny and taking control of my life. I have several song titles in mind. 'Unapologetic,' 'Unraveled,' 'Secrets.' But I've decided I'm calling the album *Taking Control.* It sums up so much of what I've done in the last few months with my life, my career…just everything."

"Wow," Jolene says, and tears shine in her eyes. "And you'll be touring that album once you release it?"

I shake my head, and I glance over at Danny as I say the next part. He looks confused as I shake my head.

We can refilm this segment if we need to. I need to tell my husband first.

I draw in a deep breath. "Just this morning, I signed a two-year contract with Caesar's Entertainment. I'll be headlining a show in Vegas so I can have a home base close to my husband."

Danny's jaw drops, and he takes a few steps across the room. "You…you what?" he breathes.

I stand, and I meet him midway as he takes me into his arms. "I don't want to go on a six-month tour that'll take me away from you. I know you'll be traveling for games, but you'll also be home for half of those games, and when you're home, we can be together."

His lips drop to mine, and he pulls back and leans his forehead to mine. "I can't believe you did that for me."

"For us," I correct, and he kisses me again.

And the best part? The entire thing was caught on camera, and we'll get to watch it again and again.

Chapter 29
Danny

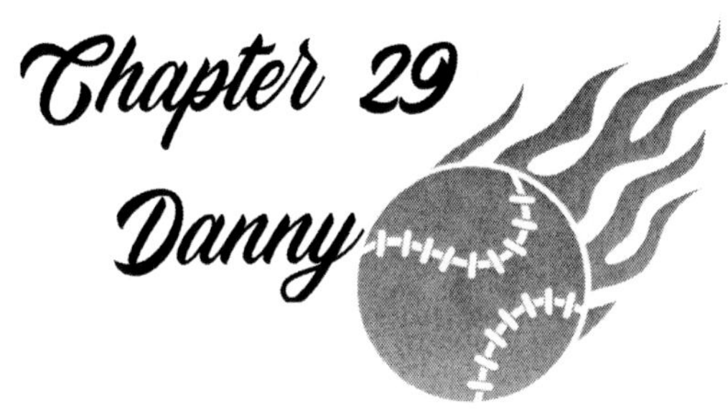

"Do you want to press charges?" I ask.

I hear his heavy sigh over the phone. Alexis and I called her dad after the interview, and she admitted she detailed how he'd been blackmailed by Brooks. We're sitting on stools at my kitchen counter, the phone on speaker between the two of us.

I should've asked him a while ago if he wanted to press charges, but it was under wraps before. It won't be anymore, not once this interview goes live.

And it's set to go live in just five days. This Thursday night, the interview will be streaming on devices all across the world.

"I've thought about it, and at first I didn't want to make waves with Arthur. We've had a great working relationship for many years," Raymond says.

"But Daddy," Alexis interrupts. "He *blackmailed* you. In California, that's extortion, and it's illegal. *He* is the one who made waves when he did that to you."

"Right," Raymond agrees. "And that's why I started by saying *at first.* Now that Arthur knows, I think he'd understand."

"And you can get your money back," Alexis says.

"I don't know about that. He was smart about how he handled this. There isn't a paper trail. He made it look like an investment opportunity—which it was, but he's a sneaky little son of a bitch. He was careful not to cross the line into extortion, at least until he offered to pay me back with the merger."

"He deserves to rot in prison for what he did. It's a crime, and I hate that he pushed so hard to come between us," Alexis says.

I'm quiet as I listen to the two of them. It's true that Brooks was a vehicle that drove a wedge between father and daughter, but Raymond did his own share of that by controlling Alexis for as long as he did. And the fact that she forgave him for that proves what an amazing woman she is. She didn't have to. She could've held a grudge. But she handled things in the way that was best for her, further proving that she's fully capable of taking the reins of her own life.

"What do you think?" she asks, nudging me.

"I think he's an asshole that karma will take care of," I say. "But if you want to press charges, he deserves it. He's out of a job, he's out of a home…he's already living in a prison of sorts just from those things. I imagine he had to move in with his dad, the man who just fired him. That can't be comfortable."

"But once the interview goes live, will we look soft if we don't press charges?" Raymond asks.

Alexis's voice is soft when she speaks. "Dad…for once, I want you to think about what you want. I don't want you to think about how it looks. I don't care about our image or our brand or how any of this affects any of that. This is what you feel is right in your heart after a man took advantage of you."

He's quiet a long time before he finally says, "Then I don't think I want to press charges. I made mistakes, and I acted stupidly. I trusted the wrong person. I don't want to get involved in a legal battle that he might end up winning because of loopholes and technicalities. I just want to move forward."

Alexis presses her lips together and nods. "Then that's good enough for me. If he did this to you, I can't imagine he didn't do it to other people, too. He'll get what he deserves."

"He already is," Raymond says. "I've had two of Arthur's top managers approach me already about a possible management division, and I want you two to look over what they had to say."

"A management division?" Alexis repeats. "Instead of a merger?"

"That's right. What do you think?"

She looks at me, her eyes wide, and she waits for me to react first. The look on her face says it all, though. We had the idea first, and she already loves it.

And so do I.

"We'll look it over and get back to you," I say, doing my best to keep the emotion out of my voice. We say our goodbyes, and my eyes meet my wife's. "What do you think?"

"I think I want to stay far, far away from D-Three and any of its current employees, but I like the idea of our own management division…starting with Gemma."

"Would her current company be okay with you stealing her away?" I ask.

"Her company has a non-compete, but I added a couple of clauses to my contract. One is that I'm her exclusive client, which Leila is pissed about but also okay with since Gemma's sister also works there so she's just switching over to her, and another is that I could take her with me if I choose to switch management companies. And switching to my own company would fall under that umbrella."

My eyes glaze over with lust. "God, your brain is hot."

She laughs. "It feels good to finally be able to use it for more than just songwriting. And you've got a pretty hot brain yourself.

It's such a turn on watching you flip from athlete to businessman without missing a beat."

"Speaking of songwriting and turn-ons," I say quietly as I stand and move in behind her. I one shoulder a little as I lower my mouth to her ear. "Need some inspiration for new material?" I drop my lips to her neck.

"Uh…" she says, and she moans a little. "I mean, I don't write songs about *sex*, exactly, but…"

"But you could," I suggest.

"Mm. Yeah, I definitely could."

I sweep her up off her stool and perch her on the edge of the kitchen counter. I move my lips to hers, and as hers mold easily beneath mine, I can't help but feel like we really have it all.

This is our home now, and I'm about to fuck my wife on top of the kitchen counter we share.

A year ago, I never would've believed it. I never would've imagined myself settling down when I was in a scoring position with every woman who crossed my path, but all it took was for me to be caught looking once at the beautiful woman who turned out to be my destiny to give me the greatest grand slam of my life.

THREE WEEKS LATER

He glances over at me, and I swear, I will *never* get tired of seeing his eyes find mine in a room filled with people.

Especially when he's all dressed up in a tuxedo.

Good Lord, he's gorgeous.

His lips lift up in a secret smile, and I'm sure he's thinking of that *thing* we did last night, and I can't help a small smile of my own as I shift a little in my seat.

I wish he was sitting next to me so I could slide my hand into his, or he could rest his palm on my thigh, or I could lean in and feel total and complete comfort just from his scent.

But he's up at the altar standing beside his best friend as we watch Cooper marry Gabby.

It's a lovely winter wedding. The bride is in a long-sleeve vintage white gown, and her groom is in his black tux as he looks at her like she is the very center of his universe. It's sweet and romantic, and it reminds me how much I love love.

It reminds me how I very nearly gave into a wedding that was all wrong for me. How different would my life be right now if I would've gone through with the wedding to Brooks instead of making the right decision and following my heart?

Who's to say what might have been, but I'm certainly proud of myself for standing up and doing the right thing.

I glance around the pool area at Caesar's Palace where the ceremony is taking place right at sunset. It's a gorgeous scene, and apparently, this particular hotel has meaning for Cooper and Gabby. It's sweet, and I love seeing all the smiles around me.

The guest list is filled with members of the Vegas Heat, including the team manager who happens to be Gabby's father. I think back to last March when I showed up at the stadium ready to sing a few songs, more nervous to meet the baseball players than I was to sing.

And now I'm *married* to the hottest one of them. And I have been for over a month now.

How is this my life? It's truly everything I never knew I needed.

And in the last three weeks, we've seen a total overhaul of Bodega Talent Agency. Our management division is opening next week. It came together quickly, but it had to so that both Danny and I could have a hand in it. If we waited too much longer, his wrist would be better and he'd be in season, and I'd be starting my residency.

And speaking of my residency, I'll be performing three times a week—Thursday, Friday, and Saturday evenings—starting in May, and it'll take all of April to rehearse for the show. I already know exactly what I want it to look like, and I can't wait to get started.

That also means I only work three days a week, which means I will get to watch Danny play at every home game that takes place Sunday through Wednesday, and I might even get the chance to travel to some of his away games, too, once his wrist is fully healed. He went without his splint for the wedding today, and his wrist is healing nicely. The doctors think he'll miss spring training and the first two weeks of games, but he can start practicing during those two weeks.

When the ceremony is over, most of the guests meander from the Caesar's Palace pool to a reception room already set up for the bride and groom inside. I stay behind to watch the photo session with the wedding party, and Danny beelines over to me once he's done smiling for the camera.

"Should we detour upstairs before the reception?" he asks.

"Why? Do you need a nap or something?"

He grabs my ass. "Or something," he says, and I giggle.

"Keep it in your pants, big boy. At least until later."

"No promises. You're too damn hot in that dress, and there are plenty of places I can seduce you down here. I don't need a hotel room—I just figured you'd want privacy."

"How gentlemanly of you," I murmur.

He leans down and presses a kiss to my cheek. "I try. But don't expect me to be a gentleman once I get you naked tonight."

"I wouldn't have it any other way." I sincerely hope this honeymoon phase lasts forever. I love how he flirts with me and makes me feel sexy while also making me feel loved and valued. He really is everything I ever dreamed of in a man.

We head to the reception, and one of the best man's duties is to give a speech. Danny's up, and he takes the microphone like a pro.

"I'm going to keep this short and sweet. Cooper and I go back a long time, and I'll never forget the day he asked me who my dream girl was. I told him it was Alexis Bodega, who I'm now married to, and he said his was Gabby Grant…the woman he married today. I couldn't be happier to see these two finally make it down the aisle after the many strikes that have been thrown their way. Now let's raise our glasses." He holds up his glass of whiskey, and everyone in the room raises their glasses into the air, too. "Congratulations to the bride and groom!"

He chugs what's left in his glass before he takes his seat next to me, and I lean over to give him a kiss. "Well done," I murmur.

"All I had to do was mention your name, and I knew that would be enough to throw the heat off myself."

I giggle. "Always happy to be your distraction." I lean in a little closer to him. "Oh, and remember how we talked about me getting my IUD removed?"

His eyes widen when they meet mine.

"Well…it's out."

He kisses me again, this time with a little more intensity than is probably appropriate for public consumption, as if my words to him are spurring him on and he can't quite control himself.

It's hot.

But I pull back.

We're at a reception.

We have all the time in the world for…practicing.

We dig into our dinners. We spend the night dancing, catching up with friends, laughing, and sharing secret looks with each other. It's the memorable kind of evening that feeds my soul in the most beautiful way.

And later, when Danny finally takes me up to our suite, he feeds another part of me as we come together in a completely different way that's even more beautiful.

It's the kind of way that makes me think about the future since we might've just created a new life out of our love. And if it didn't work this time, I've got plenty of chances left on deck with my hot first baseman husband.

Acknowledgments

Thank you first as always to my husband. You and our cuties are the best!

Thank you to Autumn Sexton of Wordsmith Publicity for everything—from random chats to working out plot to everything else.

Thank you to Renee McCleary for running the ARC Team and, of course, for everything else you do!

Thank you to Julie Saman, my bestie, for listening to every step of the process from plotting to the final words—and everything else in between.

Thank you to Diane Holtry, Billie DeSchalit, and Serena Cracchiolo for beta reading. I value your insight and comments more than you know.

Thank you to my ARC Team! I know how intense it is getting five books in two months, and you always come through with reviews and love and just incredible support. Thank you to the members of the Vegas Aces Spoiler Room and Team LS, and all the bloggers and influencers for reading, reviewing, posting, and sharing.

And finally, thank YOU! Thanks for being part of this Vegas Heat world. I'm switching gears to football standalone books for a while, but I'm not closing the door on baseball! There may be more coming in the future, but for now, I am SO EXCITED to bring you my next standalone romance, *Dating the Defensive Back*!

Cheers until next season!

xoxo,

Lisa Suzanne

About the Author

Lisa Suzanne is an Amazon Top Ten Bestselling author of swoon-worthy superstar heroes, emotional roller coasters, and all the angst. She resides in Arizona with her husband and two kids. When she's not chasing her kids, she can be found working on her latest romance book or watching reruns of *Friends.*

Also by Lisa Suzanne

HOME GAME

Vegas Aces Book One
#1 Bestselling Sports Romance

CURVEBALL

Vegas Heat: The Expansion Team
Book One

Made in United States
Cleveland, OH
22 May 2025